Anna Quindlen

Still Life
with
Bread Crumbs

HUTCHINSON
LONDON

Published by Hutchinson 2014

2 4 6 8 10 9 7 5 3 1

First published in the United States in 2014 by Random House, an imprint and division of
Random House LLC, a Penguin Random House Company, New York.

First published in Great Britain in 2014 by
Hutchinson
Random House, 20 Vauxhall Bridge Road,
London SW1V 2SA

www.randomhouse.co.uk

Addresses for companies within The Random House Group Limited can be found at:
www.randomhouse.co.uk/offices.htm

The Random House Group Limited Reg. No. 954009

A CIP catalogue record for this book
is available from the British Library

ISBN 9780091954116 (Hardback)
ISBN 9780091954123 (Trade paperback)

The Random House Group Limited supports the Forest Stewardship
Council® (FSC®), the leading international forest-certification organisation.
Our books carrying the FSC label are printed on FSC®-certified paper.
FSC is the only forest-certification scheme supported by the leading
environmental organisations, including Greenpeace.
Our paper procurement policy can be found at:
www.randomhouse.co.uk/environment

Printed and bound by CPI Group (UK) Ltd, Croydon, CR0 4YY

For all the teachers who helped make my work possible—
and for my favorite teacher,
Theresa Quindlen

*Still Life
with
Bread Crumbs*

NO OUTLETS

A few minutes after two in the morning Rebecca Winter woke to the sound of a gunshot and sat up in bed.

Well, to be completely accurate, she had no idea what time it was. When she had moved into the ramshackle cottage in a hollow halfway up the mountain, it had taken her two days to realize that there was a worrisome soft spot in the kitchen floor, a loose step out to the backyard, and not one electrical outlet in the entire bedroom. She stood, turning in a circle, her old alarm clock in her hand trailing its useless tail of a cord, as though, like some magic spell, a few rotations and some muttered curses would lead to a place to plug it in. Like much of what constituted Rebecca's life at that moment, the clock had been with her far past the time when it was current or useful.

Later she would wonder why she had never owned one of

those glow-in-the-dark battery-operated digital clocks, the ones available so cheaply at the Walmart squatting aggressively just off the highway a half hour north of town. But that was later.

As for the gunshot: Rebecca Winter had no idea what a gunshot actually sounded like. She had grown up almost entirely in New York City, on the west side of Manhattan, with vacations on the shores of Long Island and the occasional foray to Provence or Tuscany. These were the usual vacations of the people she knew. Everyone always talked about how marvelous those places were, how beautiful the beaches, how splendid the vineyards. Marvelous, they said, rolling the word around in their mouths the way her husband, Peter, did with that first tasting of wine, pretending he knew more about it than he did, occasionally sending a bottle back to make a point.

But for her family, which she had felt when she was a child hardly deserved the name, being composed of only a father, a mother, and a single child, the trips were never pleasant. Her parents were deeply suspicious of anything that smacked of nature; her mother was almost pathologically afraid of bugs, was always calling down to the doorman to deal with spiders or recalcitrant bees sneaking in from the park outside. Her father had various pollen allergies and from March until October carried an enormous handkerchief, like a white flag of surrender for his sinuses.

Certainly it did happen from time to time that there would be a noise on Central Park West or Riverside Drive or Broadway, and someone might say, Was that a gunshot? This happened especially during that period after Rebecca graduated from college, when it was agreed by people who would never dream of living elsewhere that the city, dangerous and dirty, was becoming unlivable. It was always eventually decided that the gunshot was a car backfire, or a bottle being smashed, or a door slamming to he building's basement, where the trash was stored.

This was always, without fail, true.

Nevertheless Rebecca was almost certain that it was a gunshot that had awakened her now as she lay stiffly in the bed in the room without outlets. She tried to look at her watch, but it was a small flat gold watch, like a superannuated dime, that her parents had given her when she married, as though her marriage was a retirement of some kind. It had the initials R.W.S. on the back, what her mother called her new monogram, although Rebecca had never changed her name. Still, she had great sentimental attachment to the watch, mainly because of her father, who had selected it and had taken an enormous amount of pleasure in giving it to her. "That's a beauty!" he said when she removed it from the mahogany box. "It's not waterproof," her mother added.

Under the best of conditions it was a difficult watch to read, never mind now, in a bedroom fringed by large pine trees and with the heavy cloud cover of a muggy May night, a thunderstorm moving in overhead. The room was so dark you could not see your hand in front of you. To test this, Rebecca held her hand in front of her, where it glimmered whitely, faintly. She could see it, but just barely.

She was not sleeping soundly in the strange bed, which had a well in the center into which she fell whenever she rolled over, a well like the one used for drainage along the side of the road. Rebecca still didn't know the name of the road the cottage was on. It was the second right off 547. That's all she knew. Then the driveway past the pump house. What did the pump house pump? She had said it aloud as she turned in. No answer.

Who lives in a house on a road whose name she does not know? Who moves into a place she has seen only in flattering photographs on the Internet? It reminded her of what she had heard a woman telling a friend at the next table when she was waiting to have lunch with an art book editor. "You walk in and you can't pick them out at the bar because they look nothing like their picture on the website," the woman had said. "Nothing.

Not. A. Thing." The cottage was the real estate version of on-line dating, built atop lies, leading downhill to disenchantment. Or capitulation. "We were so happy here," the owner had said in an email, attaching a photo of two men with their arms around one another in front of a large tree. They were so happy here, and then they left, and took all the comfortable furniture with them, and replaced it with bits and pieces from the Salvation Army.

A true child of New York, Rebecca thought she felt the bites of bedbugs.

She rolled over and fell into the well in the mattress, the gunshot just a memory, perhaps only an illusion. It was quiet now. There was a smell. There were so many smells. Mildew, damp linen, trampled plants. The bananas in the glass bowl on the drainboard. A whiff of what might be skunk, or skunk cabbage. In the backyard she had taken a deep breath. It had smelled as though the entire forest around her was rotting by inches.

She sniffed audibly, or it would have been audible if there had been anyone to hear. Rebecca was entirely alone. She told herself that she was surprised she wasn't more frightened by the sound of the gunshot. In truth she was terrified but her body acknowledged the fear without her mind's concurrence, the way she had developed a bad back after her divorce when she was absolutely sure she was getting along fine. Instead of pajamas she was wearing an old T-shirt that commemorated an exhibition of daguerreotypes at the New-York Historical Society and a pair of very old cotton panties. Her legs were like walking sticks beneath the wool blanket, stiff and tense. The quiet of the country was unnerving. She didn't find it peaceful in the least, more like the TV with the mute button pressed on the remote. Empty. Her cellphone would not work in the house. Neither would her computer. She had made a terrible mistake.

That was her conclusion even before the nominal gunshot, and then the noise overhead that followed.

It sounded like an elevated subway train making a turn while going too fast. Or like a drawerful of heavy silverware being emptied into a large metal bucket. Or like the pots-and-pans cabinet of a kitchen when the contents are stacked precariously and the door is opened unthinkingly. Benjamin had loved to sit on the floor and play with the lids. "Are we certain those were washed thoroughly?" her husband would say drily. Peter was English. He said everything drily. He never offered to wash the lids, and Rebecca never thought to suggest it. She was the daughter of her father, an avatar of peace at any price.

The train or the silver or the pots or whatever it was overhead crashed again, and again. The smell grew stronger. Rebecca sat up further, with some difficulty, and looked toward the ceiling. She felt as though it might come down around her, blanketing her with plaster and lath, a snowstorm of ceiling. She could see herself in her mind's eye, the flimsy blue blanket covered with chunks of white and wood. "Fully furnished" the ad for the cottage had said. Ha. Two bedrooms, one blanket, and not a good one, either.

She of all people, to be seduced by a series of photographs, snapshots really, none of the kitchen and bath, two of the view. That should have been the tip-off, that vista of trees with what looked like a stream snaking through them in the distance. You couldn't sleep in the view, or take a hot shower in it, or make coffee. Nor could you do any of those in this godforsaken house. Fully furnished. Four forks.

Not a gunshot, she realized suddenly, recalling the events of the day. She must have been sleeping more soundly than she thought not to have realized what was happening above her. She reconstructed it as best she could, given her utter ignorance of the situation. First a wire trap snapping shut hard as the lever was tripped with a sound like a gunshot. Now the noise of an angry animal thrashing around in the trap, turning the metal cage over and over like an amusement park ride. Bam bam bam.

Finally she was certain she had gotten it right. As for the smell, her imagination failed her. She made a faint sound, somewhere between a prayer, an exclamation, and an obscenity.

Skitter skitter skitter. That's how it had started. "There's something in my attic," she had told the exterminator in town, but he was too busy with a tick outbreak at the nursing home. (False alarm: a squashed engorged mosquito on the top sheet of a woman with an excitable niece.) Instead he'd suggested Rebecca call a roofer. "If you got something in your attic, it's because you got some way into your attic," said the exterminator, who was wearing a T-shirt that said YOU BUG ME, except that the bug was a drawing of an actual insect and not a printed word. "No point me getting it out, then you having to call somebody anyhow to fix the hole."

"There's something in my attic," she had told the roofer. He'd stood on a metal ladder as the sunlight faltered in late afternoon, a small flashlight in one hand. "Would you like me to hold the ladder?" Rebecca had asked. "I spend a lot of time up on ladders," he'd said, shifting the flashlight to his other hand. "Is there a hatch in your hall?"

"Pardon?" Rebecca had said.

"Well, we've got two related problems here," he'd said when he emerged from the attic crawl space through the hatch in the hall. "The first is that there's a coon living up there. The second is that he's got easy access and egress. There's a corner of your flashing with a big hole in it. He's climbing that pine tree in the back and using the hole to get in. I don't think he's got a way out of the attic and down into the house. No scat, right?"

"I don't believe so," Rebecca had said vaguely. The roofer's conversation was full of mysteries. What precisely was flashing? Scat she thought she had divined from context. The idea that a raccoon was living above her was deeply unsettling.

"Oh, you'd know," the roofer had said. Rebecca couldn't remember his name. He was big, with fair hair and a ruddy tone to his skin. His eyelashes and eyebrows were so light they were practically invisible. There was a line of pink skin along his part as he bent his head to put the flashlight in his tool bag. The exterminator had recommended him. "Roofers are thieves," he'd said. Apparently this one was not a thief.

He'd taken a card from a banged-up metal case in his back pocket. Rebecca thought his hands cried out to be photographed. They had light hair on the backs, and were covered with scars— small lines, larger circles, a big snaky one that was a pale pink and covered the side of his palm. On his left hand his index finger was missing the last joint. In black-and-white the scars would be more prominent, Rebecca knew, the hairs a kind of faint cross-hatching.

"Bates Roofing," the card said. "Family Owned Since 1934." Grandfather, father, son. Someday this man would be too old to climb a ladder and a young fair-haired man would show up to check the flashing in his stead. By then she would be long gone. Maybe by next month she would be long gone. Her apartment in the city had been sublet for a year. She'd signed a lease for the cottage for a year, too. She sighed and let her eyes close. An uncomfortable bed, a room with no outlets, a raccoon overhead. Surely she could get a visiting position at a college in San Francisco, Seattle, Chicago. Someplace where a super worried about the condition of the flashing, whatever flashing was.

"Give me a minute," the roofer had said, opening the back of his truck.

He'd baited the trap with one of her bananas. He'd wanted peanut butter, but she had none in the house. In the refrigerator there was cream cheese, two bagels she'd brought from the city now hardening into a food artifact, a six-pack of Diet Coke, a cold chicken, and some lettuce. In the pantry there was canned soup and tuna fish and a half loaf of bread with a faint rime of mold around the edge of the last slice. She had to find a supermarket, she thought as he put the baited trap into the attic.

The trap, she thought now, staring up at the ceiling in the dark. Overhead the crashing stopped, then started again. She lay in bed in the unyielding darkness wondering what time it was, whether it was too early to get up. (It was 2:08, too early to get up.) The roofer's card was on the kitchen counter, next to a list: bottle opener. Scissors. Trash bags. Spaghetti. He'd said to call if she thought the trap had been sprung. "How will I be certain?" she'd asked. "You'll know," he'd said. He'd been right. The trap had been sprung, in her muscles, her nerves, her fingertips, the soles of her feet. The house was nothing but the darkness, the odors, and the noise of a trapped raccoon thrashing his way from one end of the attic to another.

Maybe the roofer was imagining all that when he'd looked at her and added, "You know what? I'll just stop back in the morning in case we get him overnight. Let's hope it's not a mom with a couple of babies."

Was the roofer's name Joe?

There was a long silence, and she shut her eyes. Then the crashing began again. It sounded as though it was over the living room now. How did I wind up here? Rebecca thought. How on earth did I wind up here?

HOW SHE WOUND UP THERE— THE INSPIRATIONAL VERSION

The J. P. Bradley Prize was endowed in 1982 by the man who had invented the electric fence. His manufacturing company and his patent had made it possible for him to fulfill his greatest dream, which was to paint, mostly oil paintings of country scenes, houses and barns. They were the kinds of paintings good enough to be sold but not for very much, but nothing—not the house on Nantucket, not the compound in the British Virgin Islands, not the plane or the sailboat—gave him as much pleasure as an envelope from a small gallery in Williamstown or Ocala with a check for five hundred dollars and the name of the person who now had a Bradley over the mantelpiece or the dining room breakfront.

The prize he created, now overseen by his two sons, was designed to recognize an artist whose body of work "illuminates the human condition." It was meant to be the apotheosis of an artist's lifetime work, and so most often was given to someone of advanced age. It was not uncommon for the Bradley winner to use a cane, or even a walker. Several years before it had been given to a muralist who had begun his career with the WPA decorating the interiors of post offices and who had gone on to create murals for the great public buildings of cities around the world. He had had a fatal stroke three weeks before the Bradley dinner, and his life partner, who had been forty years his junior, had accepted the award in his stead, weeping through most of his remarks. The Bradley sons had been displeased.

This perhaps explained the most recent choice for the award.

The official public announcement had landed on the Oriental runner in the hall of Rebecca Winter's apartment just two months shy of her sixtieth birthday, printed on thick silky paper, like the kind used for diplomas. Rebecca had turned it over in her hands before finally opening it. There was no question: a distinguished list. Painters, sculptors, one architect, one Broadway set designer. And at the bottom, her own name: Rebecca Winter, photographer. The first woman to win the Bradley Prize. The youngest ever. That's what the *Times* would say in their story.

To Rebecca, it was now official: she was done. Yesterday's news. In your heyday, you got attention; in your senescence, prizes. Who said that? Oscar Wilde? Benjamin Franklin? Rebecca had a habit of ascribing her cleverer thoughts to someone else. Just in case there was any confusion about the fact of the matter, she said it aloud, looking at herself in the arched mirror over the red Chinese chest in the foyer: you are officially yesterday's news.

She had known it for some time, seen it reflected in the dwindling royalty checks, the infrequent engagements and invitations, the reactions when she introduced herself at parties. The stages in the life of a person who has become publicly known

are easy to recognize, from the shock and amazement—
"Rebecca Winter? Really? *The* Rebecca Winter?"—to a faint
confusion—"Photography, right? The kitchen stuff? Oh, I love
your work!"—to simple incomprehension. Slowly she worked
into campus visits a description of her career that would have
been unnecessary—unthinkable—twenty years before, when
there had been posters, postcards, sold-out shows, honorary de-
grees, auctions.

"Everyone's waiting," her agent, a woman with the metabolism of a hummingbird and the face of a toucan, had started
saying a decade ago. Her name was Tori Grzyjk, so everyone
called her TG, except for her competitors, who referred to her
as No-Vowel Tori, or NVT. Everyone was afraid of her, but
none more so than her own clients, none more so than Rebecca.
"Everyone's waiting to see what you do next."

TG was in London the night of the Bradley dinner, "scouting new talent." Rebecca was old talent, although not as old as
most of the talent in the room at the Manhattan Arts Club. She
wore her black crepe pants and a black and gold kimono jacket
and had her trademark silver bob blown dry professionally. She
wore Indian cuff bracelets and enormous onyx earrings. Her
date was Dorothea, who had designed the earrings. The Bradley
sons looked concerned at cocktails until someone told them
that the women were friends, not lovers. "She has turned the
impedimenta and minutiae of women's lives into unforgettable
images," said the elder Bradley son in presenting the prize, struggling with the pronunciation of *impedimenta.*

"That's it?" Dorothea whispered at the sight of the landscape
in the gold frame with the engraved plate at the bottom. The
Bradley sons had a stockpile of their father's paintings, and each
year one was given to the prize winner. Rebecca had been
awarded an inoffensive painting of a red barn with several blots
denoting cows in a distant field, the sort of thing that would
have found a happy home in the dining room of a country inn.

Dorothea's eyes widened at the sight of the envelope taped to the back.

"A lousy thousand bucks?" she said afterward in the cab uptown.

"It *is* the Bradley," Rebecca said, tucking the envelope into her bag as her bracelets clanked, trying to maintain her dignity. She couldn't tell Dorothea that she had never been so glad to see a thousand bucks in her life.

In her bag, next to the check, was the index card she had seen on her way to the ladies' room on the Manhattan Arts Club bulletin board. CHARMING COUNTRY COTTAGE FOR RENT, it said in sharp calligraphy. Although her ex-husband had long insisted that *charming* was synonymous with "too small, with bad drains," Rebecca did the math the next morning, looking out over the water towers of the west side from her kitchen window, and determined that if she rented out her apartment at the accepted exorbitant New York rate, she could afford the cottage, pay the fees for her mother's nursing home, manage the premiums for her own health insurance, put something into her retirement account, help with her father's rent, give a hand to her son, Ben, when he was short, and still put away some money each month for the surprises and emergencies that always seemed to arise. When she was young she'd been able to live on almost nothing; now so many people depended upon her, so many bills appeared each month. Car insurance, life insurance, homeowner's insurance. And living in the cottage would provide inspiration, she thought. A change of scene always brought inspiration, people said. Everyone was waiting.

NOT INSPIRING

"Rebecca Winter," the woman breathed, her face pinking up the way a baby's did at birth. It was like a prayer, like a sigh, like old times. "It's an honor," she added. She put her hands out to take Rebecca's. She had the kind of soft hands that are always warm and just a little moist, that look like a baby's hands, with dimples at the knuckles. She had dimples in her cheeks and chin, too. For a passing moment Rebecca wondered if she had dimples everywhere.

Then the woman added, "My mother had your poster on our refrigerator," and ruined it. For a moment Rebecca had been forty. Now she is sixty again. No, she is a hundred. She is a prisoner in the amber of her own past. "The artist formerly known as Rebecca Winter," her son, Ben, had once said, apropos of something she can't remember, and when he had seen her face he had hastily added, "A joke, a joke, a really bad joke."

She needed to reclaim the basic syntax of her daily existence, upended in this strange little town. Each morning in the city she had done a half hour on the elliptical machine in her building's gym while watching the news on a flat screen overhead. Here, when she had asked the man at the gas station about a gym he had directed her to what she realized was the local high school. As a substitute she has decided to walk, but there are no sidewalks and the first morning a truck had come around a curve, fast, veering away to avoid sideswiping her, the driver's middle finger a small stanchion in the rear window as he screeched away in a plume of exhaust fumes. Minutes later a woman with a tight white perm, a halo of hair, had pulled up next to her and rolled down her window. "You need a lift?" she'd asked. If you walked on these roads, everyone thought your car had broken down.

The dimpled woman had greeted her inside the closest thing to a coffee bar in town. Rebecca was amazed to find even this amid the hair salon (Cut and Perm, $20 on Wednesday, and she'd shuddered), the hardware store, the insurance/travel/accounting agency office, the secondhand furniture place that always seemed closed. The director of the arts program in Wilmington or Asheville, she couldn't remember which, had made a comment once when he was driving her to a lecture about how all of America looked alike now, but he'd been glaring at a gaudy stretch of Staples, IHOP, Piggly Wiggly, and Home Depot. This part of America looked alike, too, the tired tattered Main Streets where the old bank building had been turned into a restaurant that failed, where the aspirational businesses, the dress shops and bookstores, were doomed before they'd even opened. And yet here stood a place called Tea for Two (Or More), with a cheery little anthropomorphized teapot on the sign, smiling, waving with its handle, breathing steam through its curly spout. Rebecca would have counseled against the parenthetical phrase. Apparently that was the common reaction, since the woman addressed it almost at once, at length. Sarah Ashby, proprietor. That's what it said at the bottom of the menu.

"My husband said, well, hell, Sarah, you call it Tea for Two, people are gonna think you can't have more than two people," the dimpled woman said, putting a pot, two scones, and a sugar bowl in front of Rebecca. "I still don't know whether I made the right call. But Kevin's the kind of guy—that's my husband, Kevin—Kevin's the kind of guy who wouldn't have left it alone. Every day it would have been, you know, don't come if there are five of you because it's tea for two. Don't bring four or you can't get a seat. Or maybe you can get a seat but you can't get tea, that kind of thing. And I would have had to say, oh, stop, don't listen, he's just kidding, he's always saying stuff like that. He's the kind of guy, he gets on something like that, he just doesn't quit. Like more to love? Every time he talks about me, he says 'more to love.' I say, 'Kevin, I don't appreciate that,' and he says, 'oh, hell, don't be so sensitive.' So he would have gone on about Tea for Two forever. I figured adding that at the end was one less thing to think about, right? But I still don't know whether I made the right call."

"Yo, Sarah," someone said. Rebecca wasn't sure how long the woman would have gone on talking otherwise. A long time, she suspected. She seemed like one of those women who couldn't bear to leave a silent space unfilled. She looked like a Botero painting, all big curves, wavy hair, pink skin, round eyes, the kind of woman who must have spent her entire life hearing about how pretty she'd be if only she lost a little weight, which always meant a lot of weight. More to love.

There were two men at the counter. The younger one turned and looked at Rebecca until the older one elbowed him. They left with a tray of take-out coffee cups and a big bag spotted with grease. Rebecca leafed through the local weekly paper. A senior at the high school had won a 4-H scholarship to the state university. She was posed next to a black-and-white cow, holding a blue ribbon. The cow appeared to be looking at her sideways, fondly. Rebecca had never been really close to a cow. They always seemed a little frightening, like farm machinery with an unpredictable personality. Maybe now was the time.

Sarah collapsed into the chair opposite her.

"Another scone? I have cheddar dill in the back. Or some buttermilk, I think." She leaned in close. "I didn't have buttermilk so I used yogurt, which in my opinion is better. Better taste, better loft. Texture, you know? But you can't tell these guys you're putting yogurt in the scones or they will be down at the Gas-and-Go getting bacon, egg, and cheese on a roll so fast it will spin you around."

Rebecca looked at her plate. Both scones were gone—raspberry, maple pumpkin. She could not remember eating them. She could not remember the last time she had eaten.

The roofer had returned at 8:00 A.M. She had already been up for hours. The roofer had looked as though he had, too, but in a good way: damp fair hair like a cornfield with its comb tracks, T-shirt with a hint of fold marks and the smell of fabric softener, dark green windbreaker with the words BATES ROOFING in gold embroidery. He must have a good wife, Rebecca had thought, picturing a woman folding his T-shirts, smoothing them with her hand, handing him the windbreaker from a hook in the hall. The rented house reeked of smells Rebecca preferred not to parse too closely, and from time to time there was a half-hearted clanking noise from above. She wondered if the raccoon would die of exertion. She hoped so.

She had heard the staccato drumming of the truck engine climbing the hill and she went out front, where the air was fresh and lovely, grass and flowers and a suggestion of wet soil. Why did the forest out back smell of rot and the sunny front lawn like the signature scent of springtime? A glint of light crossed her face from below, like some mysterious signal, and she raised her hand to shade her eyes, and the roofer raised his to return what he clearly thought was a greeting.

"I don't even need to ask," the roofer had said when he got out of the truck, although she wasn't sure if he meant the circles under her eyes or the smell from the house.

"How on earth will you get that creature out of the attic?" she said wearily.

"First the coon, then the cage," he said, and from the passenger's seat of the car he took a long gun.

"You're going to shoot it?"

"Unless you had another idea," he'd said.

"When I saw the trap I assumed you would release it."

He held the gun by the barrel. It was carved with a hunting scene, a man and a deer, both stiff and unconvincing but made beautiful by the gloss of the wood and the faint blur to the figures and the finish that Rebecca thought meant the gun was old, and well-used. Grandfather, father, son. A family gun.

"Here's the thing about raccoons. They're creatures of habit. If you catch a coon and spray-paint an X on his butt, then let him go, a week later you'll be catching the same coon. The X on his butt will be laughing at you. So yeah, if you want I can let him go. But unless I drive him to Maine he'll be back and trying to find a way into your attic. You'll be starting all over again."

Rebecca closed her eyes. "No thank you," she said.

"Good decision," he said, opening the flimsy screen door. "Sometimes I think city people wind up watching too many Disney films. They confuse real animals with cartoon animals."

"Can I take a look first?" she asked.

"At the coon?"

"I'm a photographer," she said.

"Be my guest."

She'd climbed the ladder in the narrow hallway, thrust her head and shoulders through the hatch, and rested her elbows on the edge of the filthy attic floor. The cage was wedged into the corner over the kitchen, up against a pile of old screens and a cardboard box. The raccoon looked over its shoulder at her, its pinpoint eyes wild with fear and rage. It did look like a cartoon character, but a cartoon character in one of those avant-garde cartoons young artists were always making and Ben was always praising. Sven, the Possessed Raccoon, it would be called. She thought she heard a hiss. An overhead bulb in the center of the triangular space cast deep shadows. The scent of waste and desperation was too much to take for long. She shot a few fast photographs as the coon hurtled toward her, clinging to the bars of the cage and somersaulting as though he could spin free. He stopped not far from the hatch, and she shot a few more of his pointed face in close-up.

"He ate the banana," she said after she came down the ladder.

"I think that's a she," the roofer said. "A male raccoon is pretty mellow. He'd probably be half asleep right now. A female raccoon'll tear you to pieces if you give her half a chance."

He made Rebecca wait outside, although she was not sure why. The cage and the crashing were still, then: boom. Boom. "It's a pretty big coon," he said as he carried a bundle of tarp with a bulge at its center out to the truck. "That crawl space is going to need some Lysol."

"Can I take a look?" she said again.

He'd shrugged and put the tarp on the ground, unwrapping it. Its blue plastic was streaked with blood, although not as much as Rebecca had expected. The raccoon's front paws were surprisingly small, black and shiny, and had fallen into an attitude of prayer that was belied by the picket fence of sharp yellowed teeth just above. The morning light gilded the tips of his fur. Her fur. Rebecca raised the camera again.

The sound of a nail gun was interspersed with the faintest click of the camera. She'd liked it better when she was young and the camera made more noise. Or maybe it was simply that she'd liked it better when she was young. She knelt next to the coon and the smell almost sent her reeling back. "Don't get too close," the roofer called from atop a ladder. "It's probably got fleas or lice or something." Rebecca started to itch. She was afraid she would spend the next twelve months itching, stopping only when she was back home on West Seventy-Sixth Street. She could not think too much of her apartment or she would be undone.

The roofer hoisted a flag on one corner of the roof, a small flag that was a solid field of white. "What's that for?" she said as the flies, humming, started to land on the coon's pointed snout.

"Low-flying airplanes," he said, in a tone of voice that ended the conversation. She shot the snout and the flies for a few minutes but she could already see that she wouldn't be happy with the result. She'd been much more willing than some of her colleagues to switch to digital photography, but with film the optimism lasted longer, until the outlines began to emerge beneath the iridescent surface of the liquid in the developing trays. Now she can see instantly when she's wasting her time. Some of the shots of the raccoon might work, especially the close-ups of his padded paws.

"I hear you have a critter in your crawl space," said Sarah Ashby, bringing over the buttermilk (really yogurt) scones. "Lord, that sounds dirty, doesn't it? Sorry, I'm one of those people who say the first thing that comes into my head. My husband says there's hardly a day I don't say something I shouldn't. Never mind saying something I shouldn't to Rebecca Winter. Wait'll I tell my mom. She will die."

Rebecca reached into her big bag and took out a notebook. "Could you direct me to the nearest supermarket?" she asked.

"Oh gosh, I figured you'd asked Jim Bates all that stuff. He's the one with the sense of direction, and he knows this area like nobody else. You ask him where to find a blackberry bramble in the middle of nowhere, he'll get you to it in half an hour. I know, because in July I make blackberry scones from a bramble nobody else knows about, and it's all because he told me where to find it when I first opened this place. During hunting season there're guys who follow his truck to see where Jim's gonna set up because then they know that's where the deer will be. Hold on, let me wash my hands and we'll make a list."

"Jim?"

"Bates? The roofer who found the critter in your crawl space?" she said as she sniffed the air and then hurried into the back. "Sorry, caramel rolls," she cried over her shoulder.

"Jim Bates," Rebecca wrote in her notebook. Why did she have such a hard time remembering such an ordinary name? Jim Bates. She underlined it twice. She wondered how much he would charge for getting rid of the raccoon and repairing the roof. She wondered if she could charge it to the man who owned the cottage. She had a moment of panic and looked in her wallet. Two twenties and a few singles. At least she could pay for the scones.

"Oh, heck no!" Sarah said when she asked for the check. "Not your first time in! It's my policy—first visit is free. Well, not so much for people who just stop by for a pit stop, you know, the ones who come off the highway for something to eat and to use the bathroom, I can spot them a mile away, which I guess is what it is, right, a mile from the highway to here. But a new person here in town always gets the first meal free no matter what, no matter how much they eat, not that I think you ate a lot because you look like you could stand to put on some weight, honestly. Kevin says I say that to everybody because I could stand to lose some, but he's just being mean." She stopped to take a breath, and Rebecca did, too. She'd been trying for some time to compliment the scones, which were wonderful, but she couldn't find an opening. "But I will tell you this," Sarah added, leaning toward her. "Someday you can autograph your poster for me. Or for my mom. Oh my God, she will freak out. It's her absolute favorite piece of art of all time, I swear. I'm going to do it. I'm going to get a copy and have you sign it!"

HOW SHE WOUND UP THERE—
THE MONEY VERSION

Rebecca didn't have a copy of the poster herself. She hadn't even seen one for years, unless you counted a glimpse of it on a wall in a movie about a bunch of women sharing a house and discovering their own self-worth through yoga and sex. (In her defense, she had seen the movie on a plane, and hadn't been paying much attention.) But for years she had lived off it and its satellites, the reprints and licensing, as well as its free-floating reputation. It had paid for Ben's boarding school tuition, paid for the roomy apartment she'd moved them into after the divorce and had just sublet, paid for trips to Paris (for the Musée d'Orsay) and London (for the Tate Modern). It had paid her restaurant bills and her hairdresser tips and she hadn't even really noticed how much money it brought in until it started to dry up and then disappeared.

Her second show of photographs had been called the Kitchen Counter series, and it was seen as an iconic moment in women's art. But in fact at the time she took those photographs Rebecca had just been tired, tired in that way a woman with a child and a husband and a house and a job and a life gets tired, so that it feels like a mild chronic illness. She had been thirty-six years old and had a toddler and a husband who was contemptuous of husbands who helped around the house. "Peter is so European," women would say, and later Rebecca wondered if that was their way of telling her that he slept around. But that was later.

One evening Benjamin had had an ear infection, and by the time she had gotten him dosed with bubble-gum-flavored antibiotic and settled down in his crib Peter had shown up with two assistant professors and their spouses. That had been one of his favorite tricks, to show up with dinner guests unannounced, the guests apologetic, Peter not a bit, as though it was a test for her, to see what she could manage. "I'm surely not expected to ask if I can bring guests to my own home?" he had said one night when she had complained.

After everyone had staggered away tipsy into the night, calling compliments on the osso buco (in the freezer for exactly this purpose) and the flourless chocolate cake (ditto) over their tweedy shoulders, Peter had gone right to bed, once again confident that a kitchen magically cleaned itself sometime in the witching hours between brandy and breakfast. Rebecca had needed a moment before she started on the dishes and had lain down on their new modern couch, with its tubular frame and clean square lines, so uncomfortable that only a person as weary as she was could fall asleep there. At dawn a thin needle of sunlight through the living room window woke her even before Benjamin was screaming to be set free, and she had picked up her new Hasselblad, a gift from her father, and started to take pictures.

She never really knew why, why that, why then. The truth was she never had known, before or after. Talking about art requires artists to sound purposeful and sure of themselves, but she'd never felt that way. Over the years she'd made up a lot of reasons because people didn't seem to like the arbitrariness of the reality. They also didn't believe that she'd simply photographed what was already there—a bottle lying on its side with a puddle of olive oil shimmering along its curved lip, a handful of greasy forks glistening in the overhead lights, and, of course, what was later called *Still Life with Bread Crumbs,* a vaguely Flemish composition of dirty wineglasses, stacked plates, the torn ends of two baguettes, and a dish towel singed at one corner by the gas stove.

Her agent then had been an older man named Stephen, quiet and thoughtful, TG merely his abrasive and inappropriately dressed assistant, always on the verge of being fired almost up until the day that she pushed her boss aside and took over while he was in the hospital recovering from a heart attack. He had not been particularly interested in the photographs, or the show, but when he read the reviews and heard the reactions he'd said, quietly, "I think you may be onto something here." She'd had a lucky break when the dean of the arts program at a university described the photographs as "housewife imagery," and the head of the women's studies program responded by calling him a misogynist, and a student kerfuffle that followed got a good deal of publicity, with the female students wearing T-shirts with the photograph on the front. Within six months Rebecca Winter had become a female icon, her Kitchen Counter series described by art critics and essayists as both an elevation and an indictment of women's lives and women's work. Imitators produced photographs of chicken bones, colanders, even pacifiers and diapers, but it was Rebecca's photographs that held pride of place for years, turning up on magazine covers, postcards, T-shirts, even an ironic Mother's Day advertisement. The poster had been Stephen's idea, a simple thing: the image, her name, the title.

Once Rebecca had read an essay in which a feminist theorist posited that the word *still* was obviously a way of suggesting how empty the existence of the average American woman was, that the bread crumbs were an allusion to Hansel and Gretel, leaving a trail so someone could find you, rescue you, keep you from being eaten alive. Rebecca had been amazed at how much could be divined from a photograph she had snapped unthinkingly in a haze of fatigue overlaid with unacknowledged anger, and a title she had come up with haphazardly when the gallery had decided that simply numbering the photographs wouldn't do. She wondered what the theorist would think if she knew that Rebecca had finished working that morning when Ben started yelling "Juice!" from his bedroom, that she had parked him in front of the television to watch *Sesame Street* while she cleaned the kitchen and started a load of towels.

And all while her husband slept before waking for his seminar Images of Attraction in Renaissance Art. "Coffee?" he'd said as he knotted his tie carefully and pushed up against her while she stood at the sink, not in a romantic or even a seductive fashion but as though they were in a subway car and other passengers had gotten on behind, jamming them accidentally together. It was his very carelessness that she had initially found so attractive, as though to snag his attention for even a moment was a sign of worth.

Funny, that no one had ever asked what had happened to the dishes, the scraps, the crumbs in the photographs, on the poster. For a while afterward she had continued to use that same dish towel with its blackened edge, until one of the wives at dinner had lifted it as though it were the Shroud of Turin and said, "Oh my God."

For a time the poster was everywhere. You could see it in the windows of framing shops, on the walls in coffeehouses, in

the offices of nonprofit groups for women, above the beds in college dorm rooms slept in by girls who had never made a meal or
washed a dish.

Rebecca had followed the Kitchen Counter series with a series
of photographs of Ben, but so close in that they were geographic,
the valley of a chubby bent arm, the hill of a rounded shoulder,
all captured while he was sleeping, naked. (She had also inciden-
tally potty-trained him in the process; with his diaper off he
clearly felt disinclined to relieve himself.) It was said that those
photographs, the Baby Boy series, did for motherhood what the
Kitchen Counter series had done for housework, although what
that was depended on who you read. One mothers' group called
for a boycott of her work because Rebecca Winter objectified
children. The boycott was unsuccessful. The Baby Boy series
sold. Reproductions of the Baby Boy photos sold. Reproductions
of the Kitchen Counter series sold and sold and sold and sold.

"Please, leave the dishes. My wife will be immortalizing them
once you've left," her husband used to say to great hilarity during dinner parties, considerably less pleased with her success
than Rebecca had hoped. It had taken her a few years to realize
that Peter was an angry man, in the fashion of men who had
dreamed a big future for themselves and then had not seen it
materialize. That it had somehow materialized for his wife did
their marriage no favors. "Well, what did you expect?" her
mother said when she complained about that after the divorce.

Ironically, great success made Rebecca less and less sure
of herself, until everything she produced, even the successful
things she produced, seemed like something she'd done before.
Over the years it became commonplace for her to orient an
image in the frame and have it feel like plagiarism. "Back to the
future," TG rasped, speaking in aphorisms as though her words
were for sale and a client like Rebecca would get only so many.
But she couldn't go back and do what she'd done before. Her
son outgrew his quiescent babyhood, her marriage came to a

sudden, almost inevitable end in a blizzard of adultery, abandonment, and unacknowledged anger and envy on the part of her husband. There was no longer any dinner party detritus, no baby boy.

It has its own momentum, success. It far outstrips its particular moment. A writer who has written one great novel can go to parties twenty years later and still be treated like a literary celebrity of sorts. But Rebecca understood that novelist's secret in a way the party guests did not: the coin of notoriety pays with less and less interest as time goes by. She knew this because several years before, she had realized that she was bringing in very little money although her expenses had not shrunk but grown. Until finally the best plan she could come up with was renting out one place dear, renting another place cheap, and trying to do some work that would let her ditch the second and go back to the first.

She should have been used to the reversal of fortune; she'd been born into a family that had had plenty of money, until one day it turned out they didn't.

It is terrible, being poor in New York, or at least that was what she'd heard, although the sum total of her exposure was a requirement in high school that resulted in the collection of canned goods at holiday time, which is how Christmas is referred to in a city with so many Jews, Muslims, atheists, and liberals.

Rebecca knew very well that she did not know about being poor in the city or anywhere else, but she had certainly learned about not having enough money, which is different from being poor. Passing on restaurant lunches because the check would be split and there were certain of her acquaintances who thought nothing of a hundred-dollar meal. Agreeing only to dinners at which she knew somebody's husband would prove his manhood by slamming his palm and his platinum Amex on the discreet little silver tray. Arriving at dinner parties not with wine or flowers but with a small photograph in a plain frame—but signed! Signed! A genuine Rebecca Winter!

And in return she might receive a warm email from her wealthy hostess: they are taking a place in Italy for September, the sunflowers will be astonishing, the vines drooping and dusty beneath the weight of the black pearl grapes, all crying out to be photographed, as though they hadn't been photographed so often that they are postcards, plaques, staples of the narrow gaudy tourist shops of Siena and Montalcino. Oh, she always says, I would love to but I can't get away, when what she means is, oh, I would love to, but the airfare. How will I pay the airfare?

She had taken to riding the subway again, telling herself how much quicker it was than sitting in a taxi stalled in traffic. She was lucky, she guessed. When she had been young, going to art school, cadging salmon canapés and grilled shrimp at openings, the subway was dirty and dangerous, men masturbating and muttering to themselves behind pillars in stations garishly lit and tiled like big filthy Turkish baths. Now the subway was cleaner and less frightening and more people seemed to use it, at least if you judged by those who rhapsodized about how practical it was at parties that belied the rhapsodies because the street outside was choked with black cars, their hired drivers standing at the curb, drumming their fingers on the hoods.

The city is unkind to those with overdrafts, although it has long been their ancestral home. It is most comfortable for people who never have to think of what to spend because there is always more where that came from. Rebecca was now no longer one of those people. She had become someone who sees a plate of free scones as a windfall, someone worrying about what the charge would be for shooting a critter in her crawl space.

She had made a deal with herself: she would live here, in exile, until she could afford to return to that old New York. How this was to be effected, she had absolutely no idea. At the doctor's she had read an article about the fact that women over fifty began to obsess about mortality, and she knew this to be true. There was a certain tone of voice she had heard often in the city, at lunch or at a party, a lowered tone for the friend of a friend who had had a terrible diagnosis, who had so little time left to live, or who had just died. Rebecca actually thought very little about dying, but she thought about money constantly. She was afraid she was going to live forever, impoverished, her career a footnote in a dissertation that no one even read.

KNEW IT WHEN SHE SAW IT

Rebecca liked knowing what would happen next, and even in this strange place she began to impose order. She'd done it when she'd done stints abroad, studying art in Florence, living with Peter for a visiting semester in Rome. It had been almost like a printed itinerary, her routine: the campo for coffee at ten, the museum between eleven and two, the late lunch, the hour of exploration.

She began to do it here, too. The disarray in the rented cottage dismayed her. Old paperbacks that had lost their midsections, Ball jars without lids, random keys pushed to the backs of drawers. In New York, when Rebecca found an orphaned key, she used it in every lock in the apartment. If it fit none of them, she tossed it in the trash, although sometimes she photographed it first. In a rented house she did not feel free to do the same, but she did put all the keys in one of the Ball jars, and put the most mangled books into a box beneath the bed. She regretted the possessions she had left behind her, the big down comforter, the firm pillows, the collected Shakespeare she had always promised herself she would read someday, the cast-iron frying pan that had seen her through graduate school, marriage, and countless breakfasts for Ben. That frying pan signified home, comfortable, dependable, substantial, well-seasoned. There were two frying pans here, one tiny, one enormous, both flimsy.

At least she had begun to develop a routine for her day. The tearoom opened at six in the morning and had a wireless connection, so she started there. Sarah's Scone of the Week and a double espresso. As soon as she opened the computer Sarah would mime zipping her lips and disappear into the back, the timpani of paddle mixers and oven doors breaking the silence. On her computer screen dispatches appeared as though from another world: she was invited to an opening for new work by Iris Cohen, who had early on been described as the new Rebecca Winter but who had now come out and moved on, currently to photographs of tattoos. Dorothea wanted to come and visit before she left for her teaching fellowship, insensible of the conditions in the cottage. Ben was working as a grip on a film shooting in Queens and on Long Island. "Hooray!" she replied. She always wrote "hooray" when Ben got a job, and meant it.

The tenant of her New York apartment had discovered the air-conditioning did not work, had called the super, had discovered the circuit-breaker box, had discovered the air-conditioning did work, had apologized for all the messages. He was a retired executive of some sort, a man used to having things done for him instead of doing them himself. His angry messages were peremptory, his apologetic messages grudging. She hated the idea of him and his wife sleeping in her bed. She had realized as she was leaving the apartment, her car packed full of suitcases and boxes, that it was the second time she had had to move out of a place she did not want to vacate. The first was incandescent in memory, the day she had been subjected to the indignity of yelling at her husband to get out after a sleepless night of swelling outrage and then having him coolly remind her that the apartment was part of his university compensation and that she would have to throw him out by leaving herself.

Rebecca had bought new sheets for the duration of the sublet. Tenant sheets, she thought of them, nice, but not as nice as her own. But it turned out the tenant wife had shipped her own linens (as well as pillows, blankets, and assorted artwork) from their home in Palo Alto. "It's important to claim the space," the wife had said solemnly. She was a Reiki practitioner and had placed a small statue of the Buddha on the windowsill overlooking Central Park.

Rebecca couldn't claim to have truly claimed the space in the cottage, with its balky toilet, its rattling refrigerator, its splintery wooden walls. In front of the cottage was a stretch of lawn that degenerated into a scruff of grasses and shrubs and a steep slope down a wooded hill. If she stood at the edge she could see the flat roof of a small house at the bottom. Sometimes she saw something glittering below, as though the sun was striking fire off a metal fence or a patch of mica.

But the woods started almost at her back door, and because of the miserly little windows and the way the cottage was placed, it was dark inside a good part of the day, her bedroom and the small guest room on the other side of the bathroom plunged into gloom, the living room and kitchen lit briefly at midday and then in shadow the rest of the afternoon. It was a shame she no longer needed a darkroom; the spare bedroom qualified as one with almost no modification. She had set up her printer on a small table there. The room had one electrical outlet, and Rebecca had purchased several extension cords. She had also put her beautiful gold watch in a top bureau drawer (that stuck, even after she rubbed its bottom with a bar of soap) and replaced it with a black rubber digital watch that glowed in the dark. It worked much better and didn't need to be wound. It was waterproof, too.

The cottage was not a place you wanted to linger, not like her apartment, with its golden easterly light, the changing shadings of the park outside the living room windows—big windows— its loveliest artwork. She had loved that apartment from the moment she walked into the narrow foyer and saw those windows and the vista before and below her. The idea of selling it was unthinkable, although figuring out how to hold on to it was a constant worry, like a stitch in the side that would not ease. Its worth had appreciated a good deal since she had bought it; it had now become so valuable that she could no longer really afford to live there. Her home, her true home, her beloved home, or, as her accountant called it, her greatest illiquid asset. Most useful to her with someone else living in it. Last night she had even dreamed about the lobby of her apartment building. "Glad to see you again, Miss Winter," Mike, the daytime doorman, called to her in the dream, and yet the elevator doors never opened.

"None of your work here?" the Reiki practitioner had said, looking around at the walls, and something about the way she said it told Rebecca that she had told her friends that she was living in Rebecca Winter's apartment, that she had expected to point this out to guests: that? Yes, it's a Rebecca Winter. From the Baby Boy series.

Rebecca never hung her own work in her home. She felt it would be like talking to herself. Which she did a fair amount in the cottage these days. Otherwise she would never speak to anyone.

Instead of walking along the winding roads she had settled

on hiking, which she had discovered was both more difficult and more likely to yield photographic possibilities. She carried her cameras in a nylon backpack. There was a dry wall of stone that she had photographed from a number of angles and that she thought might have possibilities. There was an old paper wasp nest built around the limb of a pine tree that had galvanized her for an entire morning and then when she looked at the pictures afterward on the computer screen they'd amounted to nothing, nothing that made her feel or think or look twice or hard. They were photographs you had to explain, which meant they were a failure.

The biggest revelation she'd had about her own work had come one night from a nice man, a sociologist—Rebecca knew his first name was Richard, couldn't remember the last. But she would always remember the only time he'd been invited to dinner and had quoted a Supreme Court justice on pornography: "I know it when I see it." Peter had waved his hand—"utter sophistry, and so American," he had said. Everyone had fallen silent since Peter was considered to be the expert at the table, perhaps the world's greatest expert on medieval erotica, called in the student newspaper Professor Porn. But Rebecca had found the man's statement, like most very simple things, compelling, and she thought of it often afterward when she looked at her own photographs. She knew it when she saw it. And when she didn't, she knew that, too.

In July, on the hottest day of the year, she found the first cross. She had hiked straight up the mountain, winding around trees and outcroppings on the well-worn deer trail, disturbing a spotted fawn and its mother just beneath a stream that burst into a pool below a tumble of rocks. She still found the utter silence of the house at night disconcerting—one night she had awakened to the faraway harangue of an ambulance siren and found herself comforted by the city sound—but in the woods it was not so much that it was quiet as that the few sounds were loud and distinct, not the orchestra tuning-up of the city but individual grace notes. Birdcalls broken into pieces like a piano exercise, a tree branch snapping sharp and then swishing down and thump on the ground, the hiss of water coming off the mountain.

She had become more sure-footed and harder in the two months she'd been here, her arms tanned to the shoulder, her long face freckled and leathery. Jeans hung loosely on her already narrow hips; her metabolism seemed to have shifted, too, the push-push of the city given way to something slower, softer. Most of the clothes she had brought with her were useless, the kinds of things she thought of as casual and utilitarian in New York which here seemed as grand as a gown. When she had gotten the clock and the watch at the Walmart, she'd bought two pairs of cheap jeans, some overalls, a six-pack of men's T-shirts, and a pair of hiking boots. She'd run out of most of the unguents she'd brought from the city and used some cream on her face she'd found at the supermarket. She rarely looked in the mirror. She had never worn makeup except lipstick to parties, and lip balm protectively.

"She can't be bothered to make an effort," her mother would say to one of the women who came to play bridge. That was how Rebecca's mother always let her know what she thought, by telling other people while she was around as if she wasn't there at all. It was as though she had eavesdropped her way invisibly through her formative years. Her mother had a knack for lowering her voice in a way that nevertheless made her words completely audible, like an actress miming discretion: "She's going to Holyoke. She wasn't accepted at Radcliffe but apparently at Holyoke you can keep a horse."

"Does she ride?"

"Rebecca? Certainly not."

Below the stream there was an open space where a tree had fallen, the trunk splintering and then disintegrating into pale dust. A blanket of low plants with knife-shaped leaves grew around it, and where the plants thinned there was a white cross about three feet high. At its foot was something glittering on the ground, and as Rebecca drew near she saw that it was a small trophy of some kind, with a faux marble base and a girl atop, garishly golden, hoisting what looked to Rebecca like a basketball.

(It was a volleyball. Rebecca had studied at the Art Students League after school instead of playing team sports.)

At first she had the angle wrong, looking for the light and losing the image. But after a few minutes she had maneuvered herself to one side, kneeling, squatting, leaning forward. It was as it had been many times before: she could not have said precisely what made the juxtaposition of the simple white cross and the cheap trophy amid the foliage an image that spoke to her. It simply did. Just for a moment it was pure, fine, not about the fact that she had been up in the middle of the night doing the arithmetic, running the numbers, wondering again how she could get to year's end with something left in her account and a cushion for the year to come. She knew it when she saw it, and she saw it, and her heart sped.

She considered for a moment whether the image might be more telling if the trophy was standing up—she had no way of knowing that the trophy had originally been placed standing up and had fallen over soon after—but she had never liked what she secretly thought of as messing about with things, though she always described it in lectures as "manipulating reality" because that sounded smarter, more like what people expected to hear. It had become part of her story, what critics called her aesthetic, that she photographed what was there without moving, rearranging, interfering. The cross would have to be photographed the way she had found it, the trophy in whatever fashion it had fallen.

When she got to her feet she saw that the fawn and its mother were looking at her through the trees, their ears fanned to catch the sound, their nostrils flared to catch the scent. She didn't even bother to raise her camera. Nature was not her milieu. She looked down at the cross and the trophy. Maybe, she thought. Maybe not. Maybe. Yes.

KNEW IT WHEN HE SAW IT

Two days later Jim Bates came through the same clearing. There was a fresh cut on his hand just below the knuckles; it was taped up like a boxer's before the gloves went on. He cut his hands so often that he could minister to himself one-handed, although he sometimes had to hold adhesive tape between his teeth. He kept a first aid kit in the back of the truck.

He was looking up, looking for birds, and so he was almost in front of the cross when he finally saw it. A few stray poplar leaves had fallen on the base of the trophy. The cross was leaning the least little bit because a mole had begun to dig a tunnel beneath: probably no one would notice unless they had seen Rebecca's photographs, and Jim hadn't. That was later.

He looked down and saw what Rebecca hadn't really noticed until she looked at the photographs on her computer: that in very faint pencil the letters "RIP" had been written at the center of the cross, where the two pieces of wood were crudely nailed together.

"Ah, hell," Jim said. "Ah, hell." He pulled the cross loose from the ground, put it under one arm, picked up the trophy, and reopened the cut on his hand, so that it began to bleed a bit through the bandage. He started down the slope of the mountain a little too fast, his boot heels sliding from time to time in the damp moss. "Ah, hell," he repeated, "ah, hell," so that finally it sounded like one word, like a sound of discovery and distress, like an animal call.

SO HERE'S THE DEAL

The photographs of the stone wall were good. Rebecca suspected that they might be better in color; the stones were pale gray, nearly black, rust-colored, brown with veins of ocher, a tumble of muted and complementary shades. But Rebecca didn't work in color. Once she had given in to market pressure and hand-tinted a series of photographs of Ben's action figures. Lavender soldiers, apple-green robots, a wizard with a pale orange robe. They weren't bright colors, more like a faint watercolor wash, and they had all sold the night of the show. People liked color. Rebecca found it distracting and never used it again.

All her clothes were black and gray and white. One of the most painful memories of her childhood involved the bar mitzvah of the son of a business associate of her father, and a screaming pink dress from B. Altman her mother had purchased two sizes bigger than Rebecca wore so that she would get plenty of use from it. Her mother was certain Rebecca had gotten a grease stain from a piece of chicken Kiev on the skirt so she would never have to wear it again. For once, her mother was right.

The photographs of the stone wall were promising, but it was the photograph of the cross that she looked at again and again, that she put up on the wall of the back bedroom so that when she looked up there it was. The walls were rough cedar shakes, pocked and splintered, so damaged they were impervious to more, so she'd put the rough copy of one of the photographs up with pushpins. There was something about it—the simple strong graphic of the white cross, the pathos of the triumphant athlete holding a ball aloft and yet askew.

She was sure it was good, and then she wasn't. Once a day she checked her bank balance, and she wasn't certain if the photograph was really good or she just hoped it was because she needed the money so much. She'd been offered a visiting artist's post at an art school in Savannah several years before, and she'd barely bothered to think about it. Now she sent TG a message to see if they had filled it for the next year. "Bad economy no gig," TG had had her assistant respond. Even TG's hostile aphorisms had been downgraded, in her case, to minion delivery.

The bill from the nursing home was due. Rebecca moved it to the corner of the dining table, which she was using as a desk. She had found a smooth oval stone to use as a paperweight, and she put it on the bill, which sat atop other bills. She wondered how long she could continue to pay them, with no money coming in. She wondered if she should contact a real estate agent in the city about selling her apartment. She left the cottage.

The second cross was set into a swale of what looked like wheat at the point where the forest thinned on a butte overlooking a winding road below. Rebecca had to angle herself because the blue leather-bound book propped up at the foot of the cross was surrounded by a feathery corona of yellowish grasses. Its pages were flat; it must have been put there recently or the dew would have begun to disfigure it. The sun caught the gold embossed seal in one corner. "Central Valley High School," it said. This time the "RIP" was clearer, pen instead of pencil. Rebecca took some shots, backed up, took some at a distance, came in close again. She suddenly thought that the original cross, the one with the trophy, might look different now, perhaps more weathered, and she tried to find her way back to the clearing where she'd seen it. She was pretty sure she had found the right place, but nothing was there. She hiked for another thirty minutes, circling back, but the more she looked the more she was certain that the cross and the trophy were gone. For some reason it made her angry, not just for the sake of her photographs— although she had to admit that that was part of it, she'd thought of doing a progression as the cross weathered and the foliage changed—but because someone had put the things there together, intentionally, and someone had taken them away.

She went back to the other cross, put down her camera on a flat rock, and circled the area, squinting at the ground. A yearbook often had the owner's name embossed on the cover in gold leaf, but this one didn't. The two pieces of the cross were held together with a short nail, and the centering wasn't exact, so that one side of the crossbar extended farther than the other. The first time she'd just taken the photographs, but now she studied the tableau. It was a bit like one of those roadside shrines that appeared along the interstate when some teenager—it was always a teenager—crashed his car into a tree and died behind the wheel. But those crosses were always annotated—name, date—and surrounded by tributes, flowers, stuffed animals. This felt different.

She picked up her camera, took a few more photographs, then hiked up the side of the butte to see if there was any point in shooting it from above. The vegetation hid the yearbook from view, and so she kept climbing, her pack heavy, a damp spot spreading at the center of her spine. When she brushed her hair back with her hand it was as warm as tin. The slope was getting steeper, and she had to push hard to continue.

She found herself doing math in her mind, the math she did almost every day. Fifty-eight hundred for subletting the apartment, minus 1000 for renting the cottage; 1400 for the maintenance on the apartment, 1900 for her part of the nursing home charges, 1000 for her father's rent at the apartment near the nursing home. It left 500 a month to live on no matter how, or how often, she added it up. She hoped the old tires on her car held out. She hoped none of her cameras needed repair. She hoped she could produce some new work, some good work, that her work would come back into fashion and start to sell. "Look at Jane Ann Bettison," Dorothea had said when she told her she was subletting her apartment. "She was huge, then nothing, then suddenly the secondary market went crazy and she was huge again."

"Jane Ann Bettison died last year."

"Granted, but she was flush when she died."

Rebecca leveled off on the crest of the mountain, or at least the first crest. All through July she had vowed to reach the top, but it was like a mirage, or solvency, always much farther away than it looked. She peered through a break in the trees but there was more and more mountain, ever upward. Overhead she saw movement, and a bald eagle bisected the patch of sky. The shock of recognition was powerful; he looked exactly like money. He banked slightly and from inside a huge maple ahead she saw a gun pointed at him and she broke into a run, her backpack bumping between her shoulder blades.

"What are you doing?" she shouted as the bird wheeled and disappeared. "What do you think you're doing?"

"Ah, hell," said a voice from deep within the branches of the tree.

She looked up, saw the soles of hiking boots over the edge of a platform above her and then a flushed truculent face. "Jim Bates," she said aloud.

"Ms. Winter," he said, making the *s* in the term of address sound like a bee buzzing, more Southern manners than political correctness.

"I've always understood it's illegal to shoot a bald eagle," she said. "If it's not it certainly should be."

He shimmied down the tree trunk, the big gun held on a bandolier strap that cut across his chest. Beneath it a T-shirt the green of midsummer leaves had the letters SWS on its front. Under his arms the green was the darker shade of the deeper forest. He shook her hand formally but the line of his mouth was hard.

"It's illegal to shoot a bald eagle, and even if it wasn't I'm the last guy you'd find doing it. This isn't a gun. It's a tracking device. It reads the chips in the bands the State Wildlife Service puts on the big birds. That bird you just saw is the male of a pair that have a nest about a half mile that way. The scientists like to keep track of his habits. I work for them on weekends."

Rebecca breathed in, then finally said, "I'm sorry. I've interfered with your work."

Jim Bates shrugged. The line of his mouth had relaxed. "He'll be back. He always is."

"The same bird in the same location?"

He nodded. "They mate for life," he said. "Unlike people."

"Can you show me where the nest is?"

"I'd rather not, to be honest. I try not to disturb them at home. I don't really need to do that. I usually log each of them when they're out looking for food for their babies. He's out now, she's home. He'll bring something back, she'll go out." He looked down at her. She was on the tall side, but he was taller and bigger, a block of a man. She wondered if his pink skin faded with the winter light. She began to try to apologize when he held up a hand and put the other on her shoulder, turning her slightly and pointing up. The eagle was flying above them, a limp squirrel hanging from his talons. His profile was an etching, the white head, the golden beak, the pale eye.

"Oh, look at you," Rebecca said.

"Never gets old," he said.

She fumbled for her camera but it was too late. He shook his head. "I've tried it," he said, "but, you know, you take the picture and you look at it and it's just not the same. It kind of loses something in the translation."

"I suppose it depends on the picture," Rebecca said.

"No offense," he said. "Sarah says you take good pictures." He stuck out his hand again. It was wrapped in a grubby bandage. "You could use some fiberglass insulation in that crawl space before winter comes," he added. The calculator in Rebecca's mind began its desperate clicking again: 5800, 1000, 1400, 1900, 1000. The owner of the cottage had not replied when she had asked him to pay for the raccoon removal and the roof repair. "It won't be much," he said as though he could hear the sound in the silent forest. "Mainly materials."

"I have a photograph of the raccoon you might be interested in."

"A dead animal in a picture, now that's a different thing. I'll trade you. Deal?"

"Deal," she said.

"Back to work," he said, hoisting himself onto the lowest branch of the maple tree, and she stood and watched him climb, disappearing by inches.

SHE KNEW IT

During the month of August:

Sarah put up the poster of *Still Life with Bread Crumbs* in Tea for Two. (Like everyone else in town, that's what Rebecca called it. She ignored Kevin's parentheses. If there was a Kevin. Rebecca had yet to meet him.) Rebecca had signed two copies of the poster and Sarah had had them framed. One was going to Sarah's mother for her birthday, and the other had been hung on the long wall of the shop, opposite the door. "I need more art in here," Sarah said.

"This is really good," Jim Bates said when he saw the photograph of the raccoon's paws, shot so close that it was difficult to tell what they were. He put two layers of insulation in the attic. A spark of sunlight from below struck the side of the ladder laid across the top of his truck. It was something that happened often, the odd ray of light from below.

"Where's your flag?" Jim Bates said. Rebecca went to the back door where the white flag was leaning. "It fell off during that thunderstorm," she said. He put it back up so that it fluttered wildly in a gust off the mountain. Rebecca wondered if it was an advertising vehicle, like those signs along the road that said THIS SUNROOM COURTESY OF BRIGHT DAY ADDITIONS.

The shards of lights from below disappeared.

Rebecca found two more crosses. One had a blue ribbon at its base. "First prize" was written on the ribbon, but the cheaply embossed gilt letters were beginning to fade, and parts of the fabric were bleaching to a military gray. The ribbon was limp and sad from rain and sun. Over the course of a week it became limper and sadder, and she kept taking photographs. No one moved it. She thought of asking Sarah whether she knew why someone would be leaving the crosses in the woods, but she thought Sarah would discuss the matter with everyone who lived within a ten-mile radius, and that perhaps the person who had removed the first cross would take the others. She didn't want that.

The next cross had a birthday card open beneath it and was surrounded by chicory, its starry blue flowers a frame. "A daughter is a blessing / from heaven above / a gift that's everlasting / of wonderful love," the card said in pink script. "Mommy," said the signature in copperplate penmanship. ("Mother," her own cards from her mother had always said.) Rebecca wondered what the front of the card looked like. It was still fresh and untouched, although a thin line of red ants was marching across the glittery border of pink roses. Rebecca took photos with the ants and, when they had moved on, without.

The following day that cross and the card had both disappeared, and she reluctantly decided it was time to go visit her parents.

FAMILY OF ORIGIN

Anthropology 101/Mount Holyoke College
Fall semester
Family of Origin Field Study Exercise

Rebecca Grace Winter

Mother: Beatrice Sophia Freeman, born 1925, New York City. Only child, Morris (born Krakow, Poland) and Bertha (born Warsaw, Poland) Freeman. Educated Fieldston School and Manhattan School of Music.

Father: Oscar Winter, born 1920, Brooklyn, New York. Son, Jacob and Leah Winter (born New York, NY). Educated Evander Childs High School.

Mother's occupation: housewife

Father's occupation: business owner

Brothers: none

Sisters: none

FAMILY OF ORIGIN

Like most nursing homes, the Jewish Home for the Aged and Infirm was situated in an unattractive area of a pretty neighborhood, a busy street where no one would want to raise children. The residents of the home never noticed, and their families, when they visited, pretended not to. Behind it were twisty streets with old trees stretching overhead and large Tudor houses necklaced with climbing roses. From the nursing home roof the river was visible, moving sluggishly toward New York Harbor and a chance to kiss the feet of the Statue of Liberty. It was a nice view, but no one ever saw it except two guys working in the kitchen who went up there to smoke during their breaks. State regulations made it unlawful to bring patients onto the roof, even if any of them could have climbed the metal stairs. They made it unlawful for staff to use it as well, but the two kitchen workers were making close to minimum wage, so they said to hell with it.

The home itself, on a commercial boulevard, had no scenery except a back court that was more or less a biggish air shaft with some pots of dusty ivy at the corners and a few outdoor chairs. The chairs were for the visitors, usually; the residents used wheelchairs or, if they were especially lucky or relatively new, walkers.

In a sunroom with a view of a white brick high-rise a tiny woman with thin white hair sat bent over a card table. It took everything Rebecca had to approach her, although it was unlikely the woman would look up. If she did, it was unthinkable that she would recognize her only child. Not that the flat, slightly suspicious look in her blue-gray eyes would be much different from the way she had looked at Rebecca when she was a girl, or a young woman. "Some women, they shouldn't have children," her grandmother had once muttered, and for a long time Rebecca had agreed. But over the years she realized it was more complicated than that. In her mother's generation it had been assumed that a girl would get married, and a married woman would become a mother, and all of the girls with whom Bebe had grown up and later played cards had. In some cases they had warmed to the task, and in other cases they had not. It was difficult to predict: Bebe's old friend Ruth Wetzel, for instance, had been a mean-spirited wife whose great love affair had been with her eldest child, her son, for whom enough was never enough. (As for her second child, her daughter, that was another story.)

For Rebecca's contemporaries, it had been different: some of them had purposefully avoided having children, even some of the ones who seemed likely to be good parents, and some of them had reluctantly and fearfully conceived, and then been surprised to discover that they were filled to the brim by motherhood. Sometimes Rebecca thought she fell somewhere in the middle. She was not sure that she could say she loved being a mother, that three or four children would have enriched her life. But she had loved Benjamin Freeman Symington, funny little Ben, from almost the first time she had placed his bald misshapen head at her breast, had perhaps come to love him even more when she realized that he would grow up with one and a half parents, given the vagaries of his father's peripatetic personal life, and that she was the one. Or maybe she had just relaxed into him over time.

Bebe Winter had never relaxed into anything, especially motherhood. She was as definite, as unyielding, as dark as the ungainly statue of Artemis that she had placed on the table in their old apartment's foyer. There had been no Jekyll and Hyde, no Dorian Gray, no sweet and sour mother depending on the day or the mood, just what Rebecca's former husband, Peter, called the Tao of Bebe, dismissive, grand, aggrieved. How she had loved the fact that Rebecca had married an Englishman. Sometimes it seemed she even picked up Peter's accent when he was around, although on Bebe it sounded a bit as though her back teeth were stuck together with toffee. She loved toffee, and brandy Alexanders, and chocolate mousse, and the honey ice cream at Gigi's, the "perfectly fine" French restaurant two blocks from the apartment at which Bebe was a regular. "That chicken I had the last time, Franco," she would say airily as she let her jacket drop from her narrow shoulders onto the back of the chair, and somehow the poor man would remember what chicken she had had last time, or at least both of them would pretend he had as he presented and she picked.

Her mother would be appalled at the pale blue acrylic sweater the aides at the home had dressed her in today, never mind the fact that she was living in a place with the word *Jewish* in its name.

Bebe was playing the piano, of course. Bebe always played the piano. Rebecca watched her shoulders, arms, and back. There was something deliberate, even aggressive about the way her mother's bony winglike shoulders shifted beneath the ugly sweater, how her fingers moved along the fake wood surface of the table. Bach. With Bach or Beethoven she usually moved forward and back, as though Bebe Freeman was davening as her conveniently forgotten male ancestors had done. Rebecca had agonized over that anthro assignment in college. Should she write that her mother's parents had once been Friedmans? If her mother discovered Rebecca had come out as what, when she had had several brandy Alexanders, she would call a Jewess, even if only to an adjunct professor at Mount Holyoke, she would be very angry. Bebe Freeman—Freeman!—was a practiced expert at the casual anti-Semitism of the wealthy assimilated New York Jew.

Bach, Rebecca thought again, as certain as though there were actually notes and chords and movements instead of the muted sound of her mother's reddened fingertips hitting the table surface. When it was Chopin or Mozart her mother's body rocked from side to side, softer, gentler. And she had always preferred Bach to Beethoven. When Beethoven's name would come up, her mother would say flatly, "deaf," as though it was a character defect and the mark of a lesser talent. Bach's hearing had remained intact. It was hard to tell if this was true of Bebe, since her capacity to ignore the comments of others had been fully formed even when she was quite young.

One of the aides entered the room pushing another woman, slumped over in a high-backed wheeled chair, her bony head held aloft by some bracelike assemblage. In the nursing home it was typical that the patients were fragile reeds while the aides were brawny women with large arms and legs. The aides were weight lifters, the patients the weights. The social workers and nurses tended to be smaller, usually Indian. The aides were black women from the Caribbean. They were realistic, a little blunt. "She's having a bad week," they might say, or even, "I've had it with her today." The Indian women had melodic voices and were cheery, optimistic. "Someday she will look up and say, ah, there is my daughter," one had said during her last visit. It was all Rebecca could do not to reply, "She didn't do that when I was eight. Why would she do it now?"

As these places went, it was a good place. All of the money left over from the sale of the family's old apartment, after the many hungry creditors of the business had been satisfied, went to pay for it. But that had been a decade ago, before selling an apartment like the one Rebecca had grown up in had been like winning a lottery. The income from the investments was not enough, the principal had been breached, the cash was running like sand through the hourglass of Bebe's days, and every month Rebecca wrote a check to supplement it and prayed that the market would spike and the nursing home fees remain flat.

The aide nodded toward Rebecca's mother. "Don't you interrupt her," she said.

"I wouldn't dream of it," Rebecca said. She sat for almost an hour and her mother never stopped playing, her fingers moving ceaselessly. "I wish I could have heard her in the old days," the aide said. "You ever hear her?"

"Yes," Rebecca said, looking at her little gold watch. Even with her mother as insensible as she was, she had not dared to wear the practical plastic digital watch. She told herself that it was because that belonged to one life, the gold watch to another, but she had heard in her head, as clear as a Chopin étude, the sound of her mother saying, "What on earth is that on your wrist?" Those high-pitched intonations, silent now for years, still unmistakable. Rebecca's own syntax was stiff and old-fashioned because, when she was growing up, her mother had made slang, even contractions, seem like obscenities. "Honey, dangle a participle every once in a while," Dorothea had said to her one night in college, and Rebecca had flushed, embarrassed.

Her mother stopped moving, perhaps at the end of a piece, then began again. Childhood, girlhood, school vacations, visits: don't interrupt your mother while she is playing. The grand piano was in a corner of the living room, but you could feel the vibration in the glossy parquet of the foyer. Sometimes Rebecca just put down her bag full of books and went directly to the kitchen in the back, with the dim windows overlooking the air shaft, and the big table with the mottled vinyl surface and the matching chairs, to get a cookie, or a lemonade, or a cup of tea from Sonya, the housekeeper.

She'd aged well, Sonya. She had one of those strong Slavic faces that was much the same at seventy as it had been at seventeen. That was how old she had been when she came to work for the Winter family, when Rebecca was just seven. Even then she had kept her fair hair scraped back so tight that it was the equivalent of a face-lift. Not a crease or a wrinkle.

"Good you are here," Sonya said when she opened the door of the apartment she shared with Rebecca's father, up one of those leafy roads behind the nursing home, its proximity to Rebecca's mother a reflection of an assumption the world made about the relationship between Bebe and Oscar Winter as well as Rebecca's desire to make visiting her parents as simple and easy as possible. Sonya's slightly fractured English had not changed, either, even after all these years of shopping at the Safeway and screaming at the dry cleaner on the telephone.

"Aha!" her father said from the recliner chair, a glass of tea on the table next to him. "Come sit!" It was what had always made Rebecca feel loved when she was a child, the tone of excitement in her father's nasal voice. When she had entered the dining room in the morning for breakfast his greeting suggested a visiting dignitary: "My beauty! Have some toast! Sonya! Marmalade for my princess!" Then she went to the office with him for the first time when she was eight and discovered that he spoke to everyone that way. "Irving! Good to see you!" he said to an acquaintance in the bank. "Ramona, my love!" he called to the waitress at the kosher deli, ordering corned beef as though he had just invented it and wanted to introduce it to the entire room. It made everyone like him, but it had disappointed Rebecca, to know she was not special in that way.

"How is your mother?" he asked. "Good?" He always assumed Rebecca had gone to the nursing home first, made it clear that this seemed to him absolutely correct. "A good daughter," he always told people, always had, always would. Sonya put a glass of tea next to Rebecca, and two Pepperidge Farm cookies still in their cup of white fluted paper.

("Vulgar," Bebe said in Rebecca's head. "Sonya? Take this back into the kitchen and put it on a proper plate.")

Rebecca shrugged. "Bach today," she said.

"I never cared for Bach," her father said. "Maybe the Goldberg Variations, but not the rest. It was too, too—what's the word I'm looking for, Sonya, my love?"

"German," Sonya said, disappearing into the kitchen.

"Hates the Germans," Oscar Winter whispered.

"I know, Papa," Rebecca said.

"I hear that bagel shop in your neighborhood is closing!" her father said. "Sonya saw it in the paper. That's a shame! Those people made a good bagel. Not too soft. A bagel shouldn't be too soft."

Her father believed she was still living in her city apartment. It was better that way, with no explanations. Her father doesn't like to talk on the phone, never did, never had. It flattens his affect. Sonya sends her emails on the small computer, handed down from one of her nephews, that she uses to play online poker. She is as she has always been, a woman of few words. "Papa defib," the last message said. The paddles and a stent had done the trick. "The old ticker!" her father had said the next time she saw him, thumping on his chest with his palm. "Almost a century old!" Her father is actually nearly a decade shy of a century, but this is what he's always done, rounded up high. It explains what happened to the family business.

"You look good, Papa," Rebecca said. Compared to her mother, he does. Compared to her mother, everyone does.

"What can you do?" he said. That was another thing Rebecca remembered from her childhood. What can you do? Your wife doesn't care for you much, certainly not as much as she does lunching with friends and playing the piano. The family business her father passed on to you, that seemed to just run on custom and inertia, that once spit out cash like the U.S. Mint, begins to falter and then fail. The big apartment facing the park gets run-down. The wife starts to lose her moorings, until instead of playing the baby grand she plays the fraying satin counterpane in the mornings, the dining table in the evening. Your daughter finds a place for her mother, finds a buyer for the apartment. The daughter helps as much as she can, but what can you say, children aren't meant to take care of their parents, you've always insisted on that ever since you got saddled with your own. But you're in luck! The housekeeper takes an apartment three blocks from the home where the wife lives! Sonya! You're a saint, a godsend, a port in a storm!

Rebecca doesn't know what Sonya is exactly. It's a two-bedroom apartment. Is it possible that her father and Sonya sleep together? Is it possible they always have? Should she care? Her parents had separate bedrooms. Her father's was small and hunter green, her mother's enormous and aqua blue. "He snores," Bebe said. "He should have had his adenoids removed as a child. It's too late now."

"I have to get over there to see your mother one of these days," Oscar said, pointing at Rebecca's cookies and then at his mouth. He winked, his pale eyes large and opaque. For his entire life her father had worn glasses, only the style changing with fashion: round wire rims when he was a boy, black plastic frames as a young married, then those enormous fishbowls that came with disco and leisure suits. When had he stopped wearing them? Rebecca wondered what he saw now, whether Sonya looked beautiful, his daughter ageless, the apartment spacious, elegant.

She passed him a cookie and he popped it whole into his mouth. "Were you born in a barn?" her mother would say to him when Rebecca was a child about his table manners. "Kings County Hospital, charity ward!" he would reply triumphantly.

"I can't understand why anyone would boast about that," her mother would say, waving her hand.

"Sonya!" he called. "I have to get over to see Mrs. Winter one of these days!"

Rebecca was not sure, but she thought she heard a grunt from the kitchen.

In the hallway she looked at the painting above the big antique desk at which her father had once gone over the account ledgers when he brought work home. Rebecca hoped that no one in Sonya's large tendentious Polish family knew the painting was a Mary Cassatt. A minor Mary Cassatt, but still worth something. Bebe's father had given it to his daughter as a wedding gift. Not to her and his new son-in-law, but to her alone. A lawyer had said several years before that Oscar could sell it if he had his wife declared incompetent.

"The fellow doesn't know your mother," her father had said. "Incompetent! She'd murder me!"

"Papa, she doesn't even know who we are anymore."

"Doesn't matter! She'd murder us both in our beds."

"Is it insured?" Rebecca had once asked, looking at the painting.

"What do you think?" her father had replied. She thought that she had no idea.

She leaned closer. It was a watercolor, and it had been hung out of the light, protected with the proper glass. Thank God for small favors.

Sonya came out of the kitchen wiping her hands on an ancient dish towel. She was wearing pale blue pants and a matching tunic. When she first came to work for the Winters, she wore a dress version of the same thing: pale blue one week, mint green the next, yellow the week after that. The dresses had zippers up the front. The pants she wears now have elastic waistbands. Sonya wears a uniform that she can credibly say is not a uniform.

Together the two looked at the painting, of a young woman

gazing at her baby daughter, her face alight, the child's hand reaching toward her. Sonya seemed uninterested. "Come again soon," she said at the door. Her shoes are white, like those of a nurse. They always have been.

"You made my day!" her father called, and then there was a click as the television went on.

THE DOG ARRIVES,
AND LEAVES AGAIN

While Rebecca was on the thruway driving—speeding, fleeing—from the northern reaches of New York City, stopping at a farm stand for corn, tomatoes, and some beans, a dog wandered into her yard and sniffed the foundation of the cottage. He made his way from the front door, which was faintly redolent of soup of some sort, around to the back steps, where a crumb from a muffin Rebecca had eaten before leaving home, eaten standing in the doorway while peering into the woods for the source of some unaccustomed snapping sounds, lingered in the grass. A family of ants were beneath the crumb, preparing to hoist and carry, but the dog preempted their effort. In the process he ate not just the crumb but two of the ants. He wasn't picky.

His nominal owner was haphazard about feeding him—haphazard, in fact, about almost everything. One day a can of tuna and half a hot dog roll, the next day nothing. One day extravagant petting and ear scratching, the next a complete absence of any attention at all or even, on occasion, a thrown pillow or a kick, easily evaded. The dog had cycled through several houses in the four years since he'd been born in a shed near the county line, the result of a liaison between a mother mostly coonhound and Labrador and a father part golden retriever and part German shepherd. The result was the kind of scruffy shaggy sand-colored dog with aggressive eyebrows and curling tail that occasionally appears in movies or sitcoms as comic relief but that people in the country usually keep for some specific and unsentimental task.

The first place he had lived was a ramshackle split-level house where a pair of high school sweethearts were cooking meth and needed a guard dog to make sure neither their competitors nor the cops rolled up on them suddenly. They kept the dog on the end of a chain bolted to one side of the garage, and during the winter he barked all day because he was so cold. It was his good luck that one night when the temperature was near zero the chain froze and snapped, and he ran free into the blackness with five links clanking on the asphalt between his front paws.

A school bus driver picked him up on his way back from the morning run to the middle school and took him to the shelter, where he was one cage of cute puppies away from death by lethal injection when he was adopted by a home health aide whose elderly father was recovering from prostate surgery and needed company. It was a nice warm house, but the old man mainly nodded off on the couch while the TV shouted in the background, and a dog's gotta do what a dog's gotta do, and when he did it one time too many the woman took him back to the shelter. "The hell he's housebroken," she snarled at the front desk clerk, and the dog tucked his tail and ducked his head as he was led back, a recidivist.

Two days later he walked out with a man who said he wanted a family pet—the dog's file card still said housebroken, which was accurate if he was in a house in which anyone ever opened the door more often than every twelve hours—but who really wanted a dog to hunt with. He'd moved to the area from the suburbs, and he didn't know anything about hunting, much less hunting dogs, or he would have known the dog was a bad candidate: the golden retriever part with no aggression, the shepherd part with too much. Coonhound and Labrador only went so far, watered down, and the dog was afraid of the gun, and the first time the man attempted, unsuccessfully, to bring down a duck, the dog took off into the woods and ran until he felt as though the beating of his heart and the throb of his blood would make his chest explode. When he arrived at a tricked-out trailer, its white siding and black shutters and foundation latticework giving it the illusion of a small house if the light was fading, he merely dropped to the grass and, panting hard, fell asleep.

It made sense that the woman who lived there thought he was her dog, given her mental state; it made sense that he was agnostic about the whole thing, given his history. Maybe he was home, maybe not. It would depend on how inconsistent meals became, how often he got kicked, whether the door was locked on too many cold nights, or whether he got to curl up on one corner of the couch, the one with a pillow that smelled of coconut oil and perspiration. He didn't ask much because he'd been accustomed to getting very little, and he'd learned not to commit until he was clear on the conditions. Which was why he'd followed a series of faint scents—warm human, toasted bread, ripe cheese, bird droppings, deer droppings, bear droppings—up the hill to the cottage. It happened that his nose was several thousand times sharper than that of a human, which had made living downwind of a meth kitchen torture even before the cold came. He could pick up the faint lingering aroma of the long-dead raccoon and even a hint of gun residue that made him skittish. The smell that calmed him but that he couldn't name was the smell of warm peaches in a bowl on the table mingled with a leftover scone.

Rebecca would have told you she was not a dog person, although if she had told that to anyone in town, except for the city couples who came only on weekends, they would not have known what she meant. Having a dog in the country didn't require much of an investment, financial or emotional: a clothesline, a twenty-pound bag of no-name food, a doghouse elevated enough so that not too much snow got inside. The locals were pragmatic about their animals in a way the city people found callous. Some couple from Tribeca would be sitting in the animal clinic waiting room with a feral cat they intended to take home after it was dewormed, declawed, vaccinated, and neutered—after it was purged of much of its essential catness—and the vet tech would come out and say to the man slumped across from them, zipping and unzipping an old waxed jacket, "Mr. Jensen, Rufus broke that leg in two places and it's going to be upwards of six hundred dollars to fix it." And Mr. Jensen would turn his wool cap in his hands and think about the gutters, the gas prices, and the lack of seasonal work and say sadly, "I guess you'll just have to put him down." Some of the country people took the dog home and put him down themselves, coming up behind with a .22. It was cheaper than the injection. Then they went to the shelter and got another dog. Often they gave it the same name as the old one, just to make things simpler.

It was different in the city, which was why Rebecca didn't think of herself as a dog person. Growing up in a building with lots of older people, she had known two sorts of women: the ones whose faces folded in upon themselves at the sight of a dog, particularly in the lobby, who fought to have dogs consigned to the service elevator, who pressed into a corner or wouldn't get onto the elevator with one, particularly those Alsatians, terrifying. And then there were the ones who had dogs and were, frankly, nuts. They dressed their dogs in plaid coats, talked to them in high-pitched baby talk, referred to themselves as Ginger's or Poppy's mommy. The woman in the apartment next to her parents had a line of brass urns on the living room mantel, each containing the ashes of a Pekingese. After she died and her children emptied the apartment they were still there and the super put them in a box and then in the dumpster.

Even when Rebecca had a son, who in the manner of children the world over asked for a pet incessantly, *I'll take care of it, I will, please please please,* circumstances dictated that Rebecca would not have a dog because Peter was allergic. When she visited England the first time with him she realized that this was so aberrational there as to be shameful, and that Peter's father had dealt with it by always having a pair of buff-colored Labradors and telling his son that he simply needed to get on with it. In this way Peter had gotten the nickname Wheezy at school; this, too, she discovered on that trip, when virtually all his old friends called him by that name. It made her look at him in a different way and be very solicitous for a time, until finally on the train back to London he had said, "Is there any particular reason you've chosen this moment to behave as though I am terminally ill?" Kindness only made Peter harsh.

Of course by the time Ben was six Peter was off to the next woman, the new family, but somehow the dog issue had soon vanished for her son, replaced by demands for video games and computer equipment. On a bitter winter morning Rebecca was happy to sit at the table with a cup of coffee and the newspapers and not have to gird herself with boots and scarves to pull a recalcitrant terrier along the curb and remove her gloves to stoop and pick up after him with a plastic bag.

No one had ever picked up after this dog. It could be argued that it was the other way around, that he cleaned up the messes of people, that when the old man spilled milk down the sides of the kitchen cabinets or dropped cereal on the floor, or when the woman in the white house let the garbage get away from her and slide from the can, he had cleaned up after them. His were transactional relationships; he gave as good as he got, maybe better. Maybe much better. It had been a bad couple of weeks in the little white house, and his haunches jutted sharply from the sandy fur above his tail, his midsection a big concave bowl when he preferred it with a little heft.

"Jack!" a voice called from below, and the dog's ears rose into sharp triangles. "Jack, come. Come." That's what he was called, at least for now. He took his time going down a deer trail, raising his leg against a spindly pine where a fox had done the same thing the day before. He raised his nose to the sky, thought he smelled an open can of cat food. This one bought cat food as often as she bought dog food, but he didn't care as long as there was food, and the heat in the house worked.

In a way it was too bad that he'd vanished by the time Rebecca pulled her car into the gravel place to one side of the cottage. She could have used the distraction. "I will see you again soon," she had said to the attendant at the nursing home, and "I hope so," the woman had replied, but they both knew it wasn't true. Rebecca had noticed that her intention to visit her parents was in direct proportion to her distance from them in both time and space. The pink of her mother's scalp through the flossy white hair, the box of adult diapers in her father's bathroom. And the fear that someday she herself would be slumped in a plastic chair, lifting a calculator or an old cellphone to her face, an imaginary camera.

"She thinks she's a photographer, that one," an aide would say, calling her honey or dear or sweetheart that way they did that was supposed to be nice but wasn't. Or maybe if she was very lucky, one of them would say, "Somebody told me she used to be a famous photographer." There was a Filipino woman who did occupational therapy at the Jewish Home and whom she'd heard whispering about her mother, "Very famous concert pianist." She wanted to tell her not to whisper. Bebe would be thrilled if such a remark penetrated her conscious mind.

Rebecca got out of the car with the peculiar empty feeling that she often had instead of sadness, as though her body knew that it was better to feel nothing at all rather than the something her mother's playing and her father's jollity and her fading bank balance evoked. She was ashamed, too, because all she could think of was having a long shower standing in the stained tub, washing off the smell she always felt crept into her clothes and her hair during these trips, the sweetish smell of old people, a combination of clothes that needed washing and some attar of starchy food and medicinal ointments. In the nursing home it was overlaid with the smell of disinfectant and it was almost blotted out in her father's apartment by Sonya's sponge baths— the specifics of which she didn't like to think about too much— and one of those laundry detergents with a name like Mountain Spring or Autumn Rain. But the smell was still there and she could smell it long after she'd left. With her foot on the gas she felt she was trying to outrun it, and her parents, and her fears for her future—what would happen to them, what would happen to her. She vowed to return only when she could return properly, to her own apartment and a more permanent work arrangement, whatever that might be. At night she found herself imagining managing a coffee shop, raising money for a hospital, anything with a regular paycheck. An office. She had never worked in a real office.

By the time she arrived back at the house—she still didn't call it home—she was like a wine bottle with nothing inside but a few grainy dregs, a woman who rarely wept although she knew she would have been better for it. The dog might have cheered her, or at least taken her mind off her father, her mother, the money. But perhaps she wouldn't have noticed him properly, not tired and depleted as she was that evening. Perhaps she wouldn't have noticed the way his black eyes shone from beneath his caterpillar brows, the way his ears lifted when a deer sneezed some-where out in the forest. Who knows how it all would have turned out if the dog hadn't heard the cry from down below and an-swered it, hoping for food? Sometimes things have to come when you're ready for them. Rebecca Winter knew that well, was about to learn it even better.

ENTER TAD, A BIG FAN

One morning in September, just like that, there was an additional $380 in her account. It must have come from a permission to reprint one of her photographs, perhaps the combined royalties on the two books. It was an amount that would have seemed negligible years before but now felt like a windfall. It was a warm day, with a faint breeze, and suddenly everything seemed promising. She would spend some of the money at the grocery store, then make soup and stockpile it in the narrow freezer, narrowed further by the crusty ice on its walls. Maybe she would even defrost the freezer while she was making the soup.

"That's Tad," Sarah whispered as she put a pumpkin scone in front of her at Tea for Two. "He's a clown."

"I can see that," Rebecca said.

"No, like a real clown. A professional."

"I can see that."

Big black shoes with curling toes, a one-piece suit part polka dots, part stripes and stars. A curly red wig, ersatz Orphan Annie, with a hint of dark hair at the nape of the neck. And the obligatory white face paint and scarlet nose. Tad looked as though he was ready for work.

"May I have six scones, Sarah?" he said. "Assorted?"

"Anything to drink?"

"No, thanks. Make it a dozen scones. Or, no, what about six scones, two black-and-white cookies, and two walnut Danish?"

"I'm out of Danish."

"What about six scones, the black-and-white cookies, and some croissants?"

Rebecca looked down at her computer screen, studying the cross photographs, trophy, yearbook, ribbon, birthday card. There were commonplace customs detailed in the local paper that she found strange and inexplicable: seasonal corn mazes, decorated stroller parades, clog dancing. In the beginning she had tried to convince herself that the crosses were a local tradition of some sort, but she couldn't imagine what sort that might be. Perhaps if she saw Jim Bates she would ask him. Sarah said he knew everything.

"Oh, maybe I'll have a hot chocolate, too," the clown said. "But no whipped cream. Or just a tad."

"A tad," Sarah said. "Ha ha. I get it."

Rebecca tried not to look at Tad, which was difficult. It was like ignoring panhandlers on the subway: a clown commanded the eye. She had once been hired by a magazine to take pictures for a story on the vanishing circus. She had not been particularly happy with the results—too obvious, especially the acrobats in their spangled costumes and the clowns in their extravagant makeup, all dour and vacant-faced in repose. There had been some close-ups of the elephant's eyes that she had thought were good, but of course the magazine had not used them. "They're a little much for a general audience," the art director had said, begging the question of why they had hired her to take them. Perhaps for the cover line: "Rebecca Winter Goes to the Circus." That was during her heyday.

She opened an email from TG: "Don't get it." It was her response to the photographs of the stone wall. She had nevertheless had some interest from the Greifers, the couple in Colorado Springs who had the largest private collection of Winter photographs. Sylvia Greifer had given the original print of *Still Life with Bread Crumbs* to Wellesley, where she had gone to college. It hung in the front foyer of the administration building, with a copper plaque. The students had started an a cappella group called the Bread Crumbs that sang only songs that had been performed or written by women. There was a lot of Joni Mitchell.

If the Greifers bought just one of the photographs Rebecca would be safe for a while. She thought of the Mary Cassatt hanging in the hallway of Sonya's apartment. Ben had dated an associate at Sotheby's last year who estimated, sight unseen, that it was worth at least $100,000. "Shouldn't somebody take a look at it?" Ben had asked.

"It's not my concern, or yours," she'd said, although she'd often wondered the same thing. "The painting belongs to your grandmother."

"I could use a little cash," Ben had said. He had no idea that the same was true of his mother. It was not useful for children to know about their parents' money worries, although Rebecca would have found it useful to know that her own parents were going broke some years before they finally, stupendously, had. Her mother had been barely cogent when she'd signed the papers to sell the apartment where she'd once lived with her own parents and which her father had deeded to her and her husband. "You never had a head for business," she'd muttered as she left the room. "She's right, as always," Rebecca's father said, his head and shoulders down so low, his face so pink with chagrin, he looked like a boiled shrimp curved into the carved chair at the head of the dining table.

TG's new assistant—there was a new assistant every few months, the old one driven away in tears—forwarded an email from Carnegie Mellon about a visiting professorship the following fall. A semester in Pittsburgh, with a house provided and an honorarium she once would have thought insufficient but which now seemed eminently possible. She wrote to the program director to ask for more specifics.

"May I join you?" the clown asked, sinking into one of the bentwood chairs before she could reply. The chair made a wheezing sound, or maybe it was the clown. She supposed it was useful, career-wise, for a clown to be heavy. Most of the clowns she'd photographed for the magazine had been round, except for one who was very tall and spindly and another who was a dwarf. "Little person," the magazine writer had called him, but the clown had said, "Babe, let's call a spade a spade, I'm a dwarf. My mother was a dwarf, my dad was a dwarf, they called themselves dwarfs. That little person stuff is crap."

The magazine made the writer take out that quote, and refer to the dwarf as a little person. They tried to make Rebecca shoot color, but she had refused.

"Theodore Brinks," the clown said, holding out a hand and then rooting around in a brown paper bag until he found a ham and cheese scone. "I've wanted very much to meet you. I'm an admirer of your work." Rebecca's artist friends hated being told that by a certain sort of person, who was not actually familiar with the work but knew of its existence. She had seen it over and over again at shows, the banker who invested in art for its resale value, the banker's wife who wanted something to go over the antique credenza. "If only it was a little longer," she'd once heard some woman murmur to herself while she stood in front of a smallish piece. Some of the artists she knew would gently bait the potential buyers, particularly if the show was doing well and they could afford to be cavalier about sales. "Which of my work do you particularly like?" one of them might say, with the resulting obligatory stammers and silences. It would be so easy for someone to do it to this man, with his pale mild eyes. He was the sort of person born to be bullied, the sort of person for whom school must have been like penal servitude, or being burned at the stake with wet wood.

"I hope you don't mind my saying that I liked the action figure photographs best," he said, putting a piece of scone in his mouth.

"Thank you." So few people actually remembered the action figure photographs that he must genuinely know her work. "You're a clown," she said, to fill the empty space of chagrin she felt.

He nodded, pressing down crumbs with his index finger, putting his finger into his mouth. "The Magnificent Mo Mo," he said. "It's a name even the littlest children can master. The Mo Mo part. And the adults seem to like it. The truth is that most of the business side is done with adults. Today I'm doing balloon animals at the opening of a car lot." He waved airily to the front windows of the café. "I have an air canister in the truck. When I was younger I could blow them up myself, but now—no. A decent puppy takes two balloons."

"I love those puppy dogs," called Sarah, who made no pretense of minding her own business. "Remember how you made a whole mess of puppy dogs when I opened the place? I didn't even want to give them away to the kids until you told me they wouldn't last."

"They deflate," he told Rebecca in a low voice, as though it was an unfortunate trade secret. He was eating a second scone.

"And the giraffes! Those were great. And those hat things, the kids loved those. You were the best, Tad, pulling those quarters from behind their ears. And the matchmaking! You should charge. Who was that girl you found that day? I didn't even know her name and the next thing I hear, you introduced her to the guy who teaches science at the middle school, and they're going out, and then they're engaged, and did they get married? I heard they were going to get married."

"Valentine's Day," Tad said, using the edge of his pinkie to wipe crumbs from his upper lip, apparently to protect his makeup. "I'm performing at the reception." He looked at Rebecca. "I enjoy bringing people together."

"You're singing at the reception?" Sarah said, pulling up the other chair at the little table. Rebecca looked down at her computer. She had an email from the program director at Carnegie Mellon, with the subject line "Thrilled and delighted." Tad closed the bag and rose from the table, straightening his gargantuan bow tie.

Out the front window of Tea for Two, Rebecca and Sarah could see him reapplying red to his lips as he sat in the car. "He doesn't like it when you call it lipstick," Sarah said. "He prefers lip color."

"He's a singer as well?"

"Saddest story in town," Sarah said, in that way people have of introducing a story they've told before and never get tired of telling. "He was a boy soprano. People say he had the most beautiful voice you've ever heard. He sang at the Vatican! That was on a tour of Europe with the choir when he was twelve. And let me tell you, I've heard the school choir at Christmas and they're not necessarily a group that would get invited to tour Europe. I mean, they're okay, but you don't say, Vienna Boys' Choir, or anything like that. But they even sang in Vienna, and it was all because of him. He made a record, too, and was on TV, radio, all the rest. Then he got invited to this big contest for singing kids in New York City, maybe at Carnegie Hall? Or Radio City, one of those places."

Rebecca thought she knew which one Sarah meant. It was called the Rothrock competition. Coincidentally the couple who had endowed it had lived in her parents' building. They had had an eight-year-old with a pretty singing voice who drowned at a Maine summer camp.

"You can't imagine what happened," said Sarah, but of course Rebecca could imagine. Being a boy soprano had a shorter shelf life than being a supermodel. She could almost see it as Sarah went on and on, the boy with the pale blue eyes, insensible to the hormones coursing through his body as he stood on the stage at Alice Tully Hall. Apparently his choir director had chosen "Old Man River," sung not in the bass range made famous by Paul Robeson, or in the dialect in which it had been written, but in a high register with crisp consonants.

(To be fair to the choir director, he had never heard Robeson's version, or seen *Show Boat*. He had heard the song only on a Frank Sinatra album. Even there it lost a great deal in translation.)

"Like, right in the middle," she heard Sarah say, her eyes enormous in her plump pink face, but Rebecca suspected that it might have been closer to the end. The biggest strain in the performance would be on the two most indelible lines, and she could feel the boy straining to reach the notes: *I'm tired of living, and scared of dying.* That was where his voice would break, in a room full of listeners, with a panel of judges just below him raising their pencils in the aftermath of the cracked crescendo, signaling his suddenly transformed life: the boy who had once been.

She shivered. She remembered hiring a clown once for Ben's birthday party. She couldn't remember his clown name, but his actual name was Bob, and he'd arrived at the apartment wearing khaki pants and a polo shirt, dragging a large wheelie suitcase behind him. "I find that it's better if I suit up and make up in front of the kids," he'd said. "You'd be surprised at how many people suffer from coulrophobia."

"Fear of clowns?" Rebecca had said.

"Exactly." Bob had parked himself on an ottoman in front of the living room windows and as the seven-year-olds stared he had put on a layer of white, a big sprawling red mouth, some triangles of black around his eyes, a white wig that looked like doll hair after a washing. He had handed red foam noses all around, and then he had put a large one on over his own nose, and put on oversize black glasses, and made a silly clown face, and one of the little boys had let out a shriek and run to the bathroom. His mother had had to stand at the bathroom door for ten minutes—"It's a clown, honey, clowns aren't scary, it's just a man in a clown suit, it's fun, come on out, it's just a clown, for Christ's sake, Nicholas, it's just a damn man in a clown suit, this is ridiculous, unlock this door, unlock this door right now, I swear to God"—before he would emerge. "Is he gone?" Nicholas had whispered.

"It's a harder job than most people imagine," Bob had said as he packed up.

"Saddest story in town," Sarah repeated. "Well, maybe second saddest. Oh, Lord, I have to take those rolls out of the rising box. Tad is really good at fixing people up!" she called from behind the counter. "He's found I-don't-know-how-many husbands for girls around here."

"Assuming one needs a husband," Rebecca said.

"A woman without a man is like a fish without a bicycle, right? That's what my mom always used to say after my dad left. Although I was always kind of confused by that, to tell you the truth. I mean, I get it, but it seems a little—I don't know, weirder than it needs to be. Fish? Bicycle?"

Rebecca agreed, but did not say so. She was already on her way out, wondering what the saddest story in town was and how much a new coffeepot would cost her.

GET A JOB

She began hiking early, just after dawn, because of the heat. One morning she came upon another cross. It was a sad thing, the crossbar askew, and she wondered how long it had been there. Propped up at the bottom of the cross was a photograph beaded with dew. A little girl stood next to a woman, holding her hand. Both of them were wearing patterned summer dresses, and both of them were squinting. The missing front teeth suggested that the girl was six or seven. In some ineffable way the picture also suggested that they were happy, as though after the shutter had clicked they had turned to one another, the girl hugging her mother around the waist, the woman smoothing her daughter's hair.

(That is exactly what happened. The girl, now grown, often imagined, as her body was drawn down, heavy, into the peace of sleep, that she could just feel those long-ago arms around her back. There had been cookies and Kool-Aid after, and a wading pool. She still loved the taste of orange Kool-Aid, would until the day she died.)

Rebecca took many photographs this time and tried to calibrate carefully where she was so she could return. She considered trying to map the locations in which she had found the crosses. The snapshot of the girl and woman was still sharp, but Rebecca knew it would begin to fade soon. The dew had dappled the image slightly, but only slightly, and Rebecca wondered if it had been placed there just that morning, just before she came upon it, and she looked around her. But no one was there, not a soul.

As she walked on she heard a faint slithering sound behind her; the cross had fallen into two pieces, the crossbar falling atop the photograph. She went back and took more shots. There was something, she told herself. There was something here. As she looked at the image she felt both satisfaction and sadness. The girl still squinted against the strength of some long-ago sunlight, but the woman had disappeared, the crossbar obscuring her face.

Rebecca had never spent much time with other photographers; Peter didn't like it, which she had been dumb enough to find flattering. But when she was on panels or at openings, her male colleagues made their work sound like either hard manual labor—ladders, treks, small planes, hours and hours and shot after shot—or stupendous alchemy of which, unspoken, their genius was the greatest part. Rebecca had never seen it that way. She mainly found her good work to be accidental, and immediate. She shot Ben's red toy truck, the garlic press and the cutting board, the section of the stone wall with the gap that registered black and ominous in the photograph. And somehow, sometimes, it worked.

That's what she felt when she looked at the cross photographs.

She had not labored over them, or transformed them with the gift of her eye, at least not so she could tell. She just felt them. If no one wanted these photographs she would break her own rule and hang them on her own walls. If she ever had her own walls again. 5800. 1000. The numbers, so often considered that they had become automatic, never changed. She hoped someone would want these photographs. "Don't get it," TG might say, but she would be wrong.

The next day Rebecca got a job.

SITTING IN A TREE

Turned out the main difference between sitting in a tree stand waiting for a deer with a gun and sitting in a tree stand waiting for raptors with a chip reader and a camera is conversation. You can't make conversation while waiting for the deer. You can't even smoke a cigarette if you are so inclined. You can have some coffee if you're very careful about clinking the thermos and your arm motions are very slow and precise. But mainly you sit and wait for a buck to enter the clearing and bend his antlered head to the stream to drink, looking for a clear shot so that you don't wound the poor guy and watch as he crashes, bloodied, into the undergrowth and the far environs, there to die, useless, instead of parceled by the butcher on old Route 127 into neat vacuum-packed packages with preprinted stickers: loin, chops, steaks, venison sausage, venison bologna.

Thus sayeth Jim Bates.

"Now, that's completely different than when my dad and his brothers hunted," he said after telling her that speech was acceptable if it was muted. "They'd field-dress it where it fell, then bring the deer back to our garage and finish the job. My uncle Fred put a trough sink on one wall and ran a water line direct to our septic just so they could butcher and clean. Then they'd package the meat themselves in brown paper and string. It's neater now, but it loses something in the translation. There's nothing like eating a piece of meat you've butchered yourself."

Rebecca didn't know what to say. Nothing in the last ten minutes of conversation was within her ken: the deer, the kill, the butchering, even the venison, which occasionally showed up as a novelty on the menu of some three-star restaurant but which she had certainly never prepared herself. She had also never expected to share the close quarters of a tree stand with a man who she suspected was wearing Old Spice and who would blithely utter the sentence, "There's nothing like eating a piece of meat you've butchered yourself."

Just as Rebecca was attempting to frame a reply—with great difficulty, having never eaten a piece of meat she'd butchered herself—there was the sound of something tearing through the rough shrubbery at the edge of the clearing. A man in a cap and a mustard-brown canvas coat emerged trailing a small boy. The man looked up into the tree. The boy sniffed loudly. His nose was a mess. It was all Rebecca could do not to pull a tissue from her jacket pocket and float it down from the tree stand to his snotty hand.

"Jim," the man said.

"Bill," said Jim as the man jabbed the boy in the back. The boy's face closed like the shutter of a camera. He wiped his nose with his hand. His father looked from Jim to Rebecca and back again so conspicuously that his head actually swiveled. She wasn't sure, but Rebecca even thought she heard him say "Hunh."

"Janice good?" Jim Bates finally said.

"She's getting over the shingles," the man said, looking away, the barrel of a long gun poking from a sling on his back.

"I hear that's really painful," Jim said.

"Do many people pass through here?" Rebecca said when the man and boy had moved on.

"No. They're just scouting deer trails so they'll know where to set up to hunt."

There was an entire world out there about which she knew nothing. Field-dress. Trough sink. A language she suspected she had encountered only in nineteenth-century American novels. This man was sure of himself in this language. It was his native tongue. He wasn't sure of himself the way her husband had been, with an overlay of condescension. After three hours in a tree beside him, she knew he was simply a guy who knew things, just as Sarah had said. She imagined that the things he didn't know he didn't feel the need to know.

It had turned out that climbing a tree was more difficult than it looked. It was harder than warrior pose in yoga, than teaser in Pilates, than the elliptical or the Reformer. Rebecca thought that if no one had thought of it yet, soon enough someone in the city would spearhead a craze for tree climbing in Central and Prospect Parks, and it would become the talk of every cocktail party: have you tried that large oak by the Sheep Meadow? Oh, it's completely changed my body.

"You need a boost?" Jim Bates had asked.

"I'm fine," Rebecca said as she scrambled inelegantly onto the lowest branch, which was not low enough.

He'd been parked in front of the cottage when she returned from her morning hike the week before. Sarah had said he was replacing the slate roof on an old church in Connecticut. "The man works!" Sarah said. The part in his pale hair was sunburnt.

"I've got a proposition for you," he'd said. "The state wildlife guy wants to put together something to get more money for his agency, and he thinks he'll do better if I make up some maps and he's got some pictures to go with them. I said I knew somebody who might take some pictures."

"Does he know who I am?" Rebecca had asked, and then felt foolish.

"I just said I knew someone with experience. They'll pay two hundred dollars a day. The catch is, I can only do it weekends because of this roofing job I'm doing."

The catch is, Rebecca thought, that that's less than what I used to spend on car service. One way. It's less than I once spent on film for a shoot when I still used film. Less than I would pay for an art school assistant on a busy day.

"Will the rights to the photographs revert to me after they use them?"

"Oh, man, you got me. Want me to ask and let you know?"

She thought for a moment. 5800. 1000. 200. 200. "I'll do it," she said.

Sitting in a tree, in a tree stand, a term of art with which she was also unfamiliar. "Did you build the tree house?" she had asked, her feet finally on solid ground, no longer feeling for purchase on a branch, and he'd laughed. "You're not a hunter," he said.

The tree was at the edge of a small clearing with a stream running through it. A muddy trampled patch by a stand of rocks showed where the deer came to drink and then cross into the deeper woods. There were faded folding canvas stools in the tree stand. "Sometimes you have to sit here for hours before you get your buck," Jim Bates said. "You might as well get comfortable."

"You wouldn't attempt to shoot a deer while we're waiting for the birds?"

He smiled again. "Hunting season starts the Monday after Thanksgiving. You should figure on staying inside that week as much as you can, and wearing orange if you have to go out. Do you eat venison? I can bring you some."

Rebecca had never eaten venison, but her first thought was

that it was free food, and her second that it was uniquely humiliating that that was the first thought to cross her mind. She brought her lips together and nodded. "That would be nice," she said.

"Don't do me any favors," he said.

She felt herself redden, embarrassed. "No, I would appreciate that."

"Some people make it through the whole winter without buying meat at the market," he said, standing up and lifting his tracking gun to the window of sky he'd created by sawing off a large branch. Rebecca rose next to him. There was a high cry, a single harsh complaining note, and a hawk soared over the trees on the other side of the clearing. Both of them pointed and shot.

"I'm not very good at this sort of photography," Rebecca said.

He wrapped his hand around her arm, and Rebecca drew back slightly. But she realized he had only wanted her to keep still for a moment. The first cry faded, another grew louder, and the hawk landed hard by the stream. It turned its head as though it was looking at them. As she trained her camera on the bird it occurred to her that she had known much of life in two dimensions: raccoon, eagle. She had learned to know what things looked like but not what they really amounted to. This three-dimensional life was completely different. The hawk looked her right in the eye and it was as though she was seeing the bird, really seeing it, for the first time.

Jim Bates scribbled in a notebook. "That one's already tagged," he said, reading his notes. "Male red-tailed hawk, at least three years old. Now we've got a picture of him, too. The state wildlife people are getting their money's worth."

There was not much to see or photograph during the rest of the morning. The same hawk circled back. A Cooper's hawk flew over. "Chicken hawks, they used to call them," Jim said. "I don't know why they picked on those guys, since all hawks will take a chicken, usually without even slowing down."

Rebecca looked at her camera. The Cooper's hawk had an intricate geometric pattern to its dusky feathers, and in the photographs you could see it perfectly. Once again she had the odd sense that she had been missing something, seeing the world flat when everything was rounded. Sitting quietly in the tree stand, she wondered if that was what moved her about the cross photographs, that the crosses themselves and the suggestion of the person who'd placed them were more than images, more like a story. Maybe that was what people had seen in the Kitchen Counter series, a story. But it was their story, not her own.

A big bird Jim thought was an osprey passed overhead, but there was no warning and neither of them got a clear shot. They shared some scones and a thermos of coffee. It was the first time she had had coffee with sugar since college. It was the first time she understood how the people who now lived around her seemed to feel about their surroundings. From up in the tree stand she felt as if she owned all of this, the land, the trees, the big stones caressed by the water of the stream, the birds, the deer, the squirrels, the chipmunks. You were just far enough above it to feel as though you held sway. Up in a plane you felt as though you weren't even part of the land, the small commas of blue swimming pool, the big rectangles of cornfield, the flat Monopoly board vistas of housing developments. On the ground you felt like nothing, like just another bit of it all. But up here, you felt like you were in it, like you owned it even if you had no idea who did.

"Who owns this land?" she asked.

"The water company," Jim said.

A couple hours in he put his hand over his heart and took out a cellphone. He peered at the screen, then muttered, "Sorry," and turned his back. It was like being in an airplane before take-off and pretending not to hear the phone conversation of the passenger in the next seat. "That's because you leave the windows open," he said at one juncture, and later, "I can't get down there right now, but I'll get there before dinner and take care of it. Just close the bathroom door. He's more afraid of you than you are of him."

"Your wife?" Rebecca said after he hung up.

"My sister. I'm not married. Not anymore. You?"

"If I were married it would be a little peculiar if I were living here by myself."

"My father used to say the world is full of peculiar," he said. "I think we'll call it a day."

"I've only got good photographs of two birds," she said.

"They're paying you by the day, not by the bird," he said.

Getting down was, in some fashion, more difficult than getting up. She sat on the last branch, looking at the ground below. It reminded her of swimming from the boat to the beach, but in reverse: the beach always looked closer than it really was, while here she was certain it could not be as far down as it appeared.

"Just drop," he said, and he caught her and lowered her to the ground.

"You could use some venison," he said, walking away into the forest while she pulled her shirt straight and pushed her hair behind her ears. "Or a grilled cheese sandwich. I make a good grilled cheese sandwich."

A GOOD GRILLED
CHEESE SANDWICH

"I make a good grilled cheese sandwich," Jim Bates said again
an hour later, Rebecca sitting a little uneasily in his tidy kitchen,
with its gold cabinets and flowered wallpaper and pale yellow
Formica, a kitchen frozen in 1967. As was Jim Bates's grilled
cheese sandwich:

> *Take two slices of Wonder bread.*
> *Spread each with a lot of butter.*
> *Put three slices of Velveeta between them.*
> *Cook in a frying pan on both sides until brown and oozing.*

"No wonder," she said.
"What's that supposed to mean?"
"Two tablespoons of butter?"

"You don't want it to stick to the pan."

"It's a nonstick pan."

"Still," he said, popping the tops off two beers.

"What about your arteries?"

"My arteries are fine. Your arteries are fine. Look at you. You want another one? I'm thinking of having another one."

"No. No thank you. Don't you find it impossible to cook anything decent on an electric stove?"

"Don't you have an electric stove?"

"There's one in the house I'm renting. That's why I ask."

"What about in your real place?" he asked.

Your real place. That's what it is, Rebecca thought. Isn't it? My real place. Oh.

"I have a gas stove there." A six-burner cast-iron white-enameled gas stove that, at this moment in her life, Rebecca could not quite believe she had once paid six thousand dollars to acquire. And that figure did not include the cost of having it disassembled and then assembled again, since naturally it was too large to fit through the door of the kitchen. It was a common problem in Manhattan, the subject of many amused stories at parties and lunches. We bought this couch/armoire/desk/stove. And it wouldn't fit through the door.

Using the lens of this place, much of her past seemed so improbable. She could imagine this man saying, "You can get a perfectly good stove for six hundred dollars. You can measure it first to make sure you can get it in the house. I've got a tape measure in the truck."

"My mother cooked pretty decent meals almost every night on an electric stove until I was eighteen," Jim Bates said, flipping his second sandwich. "I'd put her meat loaf up against anybody's."

"And after you were eighteen?"

"She died. That's when I started making grilled cheese for my sister."

"I'm sorry," said Rebecca.

"It was a long time ago," Jim Bates said, sitting down. "You still have your parents?"

"Yes."

"Both?"

"Yes." After a fashion, Rebecca wanted to add, picturing her mother playing "Für Elise" on a plastic cafeteria tray after sweeping the food to the floor amid the cries of the staff.

"You're lucky," he said, with his mouth full.

He seemed like a nice man, Rebecca thought, but she knew better than to use those words. Ever since Hallie Cohen—third of four, older brother and sister, younger brother who admittedly was a bit of a brat—had sat in Rebecca's airless and noiseless bedroom and said, "You're lucky," Rebecca had been suspicious of the sentiment, and the intervening years had proved her correct. You're so lucky, to the couple at an anniversary party who, in private, scarcely spoke. You're so lucky, to the young mother who heard a stirring and cry at night from the crib and swore she would lose her mind. Lucky from the outside was an illusion. Jim Bates had lost his mother when she still walked upright, when she still took word retrieval and continence for granted, when she cared for him and not the other way around.

Had all that feeling rippled across her still face? All she knew was that once he swallowed and swabbed his mouth with a paper towel, Jim Bates added, "I probably shouldn't assume, right? My father used to say you should never assume."

"Because it makes an ass out of you and me," Rebecca said.

"So my old man wasn't the only guy who said that, huh?"

"Until this very moment, I assumed—oh, goodness, there I go, see?—I assumed my father was the only person on earth who actually used that expression. In fact when I was a child I may have even assumed he invented it."

"I'm pretty sure not. We were in one of those tourist shops by

Niagara Falls and we saw some kind of plaque that had it on it. I wanted to buy it but my mom said it was too expensive. Your father ever tell you there's no *I* in *team*? My father loved that one, too."

Rebecca shook her head. "No. But sometimes he would whisper, *'Mann tracht und Gott lacht.'* 'Man plans, God laughs.'"

"Your father spoke German?"

"It's complicated."

"Right," Jim Bates said, eating the end of his sandwich. "You sure you don't want another one?"

CUCUMBER SANDWICHES

Sarah was always trying to fix Jim Bates up. She'd tried to fix him up with the woman who drove the truck that brought her bulk flour and shortening, and the woman who ran the print shop out of her house and printed Sarah's menus, and even the weekend bartender at Ralph's, a beautician who was kind of skanky, with her cutoffs and halter tops, but by that time Sarah was down to saying to Kevin, "Maybe the poor guy just needs a one-night stand."

"Guy can take care of himself," Kevin said, lying back on the sofa, balancing turkey on a croissant on his belly. "Can't a guy ever get a plain piece of bread around here?" he said sometimes.

Sarah loved Jim Bates, but not in a romantic fashion, since she had an undoubted thing for unpleasant men who treated her badly. Jim had been just the opposite. He'd been the only person willing to sit her down and tell her why her business was failing, and he did it soon enough that she could turn things around. She'd set up as an English tearoom, which had been her dream since she was a little girl and had read a series of books about three children who lived in an English manor house and had adventures with talking animals. Trifle, treacle, toad-in-the-hole—Sarah never forgot the foods they had at tea, or the fact that they had tea at all, and that it wasn't something to drink but an entire meal. Her mother had made her major in marketing at the state university so she would be able to support herself—"instead of assuming some man will do it," said her mother, who never got over her bitterness at her divorce.

But what Sarah really wanted to do was move to England, where everything was better: china, gardens, accents, Shakespeare plays. Then she met Kevin her senior year, and decided what she would do instead was be a mother who read those books about the English children to her own, and ran an English business of some kind or another. After she spent a summer working at a bakery near campus she decided on an English tearoom. Kevin got a job selling cars in a lot off the interstate, and they settled in Squamash, which everyone said was going to be the next place the city people came to spend the weekend. Only they didn't, not really, although there were a few of them who bought houses on the outskirts with plenty of land because it was cheaper than the more popular places.

Sarah got herself some tiered porcelain serving dishes with flowers twining around the fluted edges, and some teapots with cozies made to look like little old women, and a small business loan that she figured she could manage each month with the marketing plan she'd learned in her advanced marketing class. She gave away free samples the first week and people sniffed the air outside the shop appreciatively and smiled and told her they'd be back. And they were, for about two weeks, and then they weren't.

"What'd I tell you about a burger place?" Kevin said. "Everybody likes a burger."

"I don't care about burgers," Sarah replied.

Week three and Jim Bates came in and sat in one of her little spindly bentwood chairs. She'd seen him twice before, but she'd never noticed how big he was, or how inadequate the chairs looked holding a person of his size. He was a man who liked sugar; he ordered cocoa and a maple pecan scone. "You make a good scone," he said.

"Thank you," she said, and her dimpled chin quivered, and tears began to run down her face.

"It's like that, huh?" he said, looking around at the little tables and tiny chairs, all empty.

It wasn't what he said, that's for sure. It was his tone of voice, kind of even, soothing. "You know why, right?" Kevin said that night, thinking like he always did that any man who was nice to a woman wanted to sleep with her, and would stop being nice as soon as he had. But Jim Bates wasn't like that. He was just a nice man who told her that Squamash wasn't ready for cucumber and watercress sandwiches or oolong tea, that if she could see her way clear to making good strong coffee and even offering it in take-out cups, that if she could learn to make a cheese Danish and a sticky bun, there would be lines at the register first thing in the morning. He told her that there was no reason she couldn't make nice sandwiches, but that they'd have to be bigger than a pack of matches and the bread not spread with unsalted butter. He told her that maybe there was room on her menu for a section called English Specialties, and that if she explained what bangers and mash were she could even sell some because he knew for a fact that there were plenty of guys in the area who liked both sausages and mashed potatoes as long as they knew that's what they were ordering.

He'd been right about everything. She thought he was the kindest guy she'd ever known. Much much nicer than her father, who never even bothered with a birthday card after he left, or her brother, who referred to her as "fat ass" when they were young and called only when he wanted to borrow money. Much nicer, although she would be the last to admit it, than Kevin, who always had to go out at night and meet with someone or other now that he had quit the car lot—"bunch of losers"—and become what he called an entrepreneur, buying truckloads of firewood and reselling it in overpriced cords to flower shops and gourmet stores in neighboring towns (who then marked the price up even further for the weekend people).

Kevin didn't like Jim Bates and Sarah couldn't figure out why, but that's because she hadn't been at Ralph's the night Kevin was playing pool and making jokes about Sarah. They all sounded like old jokes, the kind that seventy-five-year-old comedians made on television: my wife is so fat she has her own zip code. My wife is so fat that when she wears yellow in New York people try to hail her. My wife is so fat she brought a spoon to the Super Bowl. Kevin was the only guy laughing at the jokes, laughing hard, like a cross between a cough and a bark, and he was in midlaugh when Jim Bates, who had been having a beer with a siding guy and working out a schedule on a building project, walked by and said, "It would be good if you stopped insulting your wife in front of strangers."

"Who the hell do you think you are?" Kevin had said, looking down the length of the bar and then at the bartender, who was stocking the beer fridge and didn't look up.

"It would be good," Jim said.

"Mind your own damn business," Kevin said, and from one of the tables in the dim back of the bar someone muttered, "At least he's got a business."

"What?" But everyone was looking innocent and Jim Bates was walking out. Not everyone liked him, mainly because they recognized in him a man who didn't cut corners or do deals under the table. But virtually all of them had roofs on their houses, which meant Jim was indispensable, while Kevin was an outsider and a known scamster.

"Hey!" Kevin called, and finally the bartender looked up. "Leave it alone," said the bartender, who had played catcher in high school when Jim Bates was shortstop.

"Asshole."

"Pay your tab and call it a night," the bartender said.

Kevin had stopped making comments about Sarah's weight, and her hair, and her chin and her conversation, when other people were around. But it didn't stop him from doing it at home. Jim Bates sometimes thought he should have the kind of conversation with Sarah about her marriage that he'd had with her about her business, but he was smart enough to know that downing watercress sandwiches and downing a woman's husband were two different things. He, too, had once been married to someone to whom he had felt mysteriously and irrationally attached, until she'd unattached herself.

Sarah kept trying to fix Jim Bates up. She'd write names and phone numbers on paper napkins and tuck them into the little flowered folder with his lunch check inside. He'd put the napkins in his pockets, and then on Sunday afternoons, when he did the laundry, he'd toss them in the trash, along with the occasional Sheetrock nail.

But Sarah never thought of fixing him up with Rebecca.

"One, she's too famous and sophisticated, and, two, she's too old for him."

"Maybe the old ones are more willing to go along," Kevin said. "Besides, she doesn't look that old. She looks better than most of the forty-year-olds around here. She probably does one of those exercise deals." Sarah hoped he wasn't going to start in on her again. She knew she should work out but she started baking every morning at five. She figured they were never going to have children because Kevin never wanted to have sex.

(At least not with Sarah. Jim had wadded up the napkin with

the skanky weekend bartender's number on it with particular venom and lobbed it into the toilet by the washer because he knew she and Kevin hooked up at her apartment at least once a week.)

"She isn't good-looking, I gotta say," Kevin added. "She's got that long face and that weird mouth."

"Oh, you're so wrong. She's beautiful. Not in that kind of cheerleader way, but she has such a strong face. The mouth is the best part of it."

Kevin shrugged. "I don't see it, but what do I know? Maybe it's one of those things women like and guys don't, like, I don't know, sweaters?"

"Guys don't like sweaters?" Sarah said.

"Nah. Guys like shirts. Girls like sweaters."

REBECCA'S MOUTH

It so happened that while Jim Bates did not like sweaters—he always found them itchy and preferred flannel shirts and old T-shirts laundered to near-tissue—he had come to admire Rebecca's mouth. At first he had found it strange. It was very wide, with a strongly delineated upper lip that looked as though it had been drawn with a sharp pencil. The lower lip was completely different, thick and slightly drooping, and in recent years young female photographers had speculated about whether Rebecca had had it plumped up for reasons of vanity. In fact she had had it all her life; in baby pictures it made her look a little simple-minded, and her mother had told everyone that she had no idea what part of the family had a mouth like that but she assumed it must be her husband's.

When Rebecca was in art school one of her classmates had

asked to paint her, and he had made her mouth the centerpiece of the painting, enormous and epicene. It was cruel, her small eyes and slightly pointed nose crowded to the center of what was, after all, a rather long face, all completely obliterated by the huge lips across the center of the canvas. But Rebecca was forced to be of two minds about the painting, which showed her in a yellow turtleneck—although of course the one she had worn for the sittings was black—with a long braid of hair slithering down one shoulder, reminiscent of the Modigliani *Girl with Braids*. As a personal matter she was slightly insulted and re-pelled by it, but as a professional one she knew it was very fine, and the young painter, Josef Gourdon, would go on to become as famous a portraitist as Rebecca was a photographer. "My muse!" he would cry extravagantly at a gallery or a gala, his arm around whichever young male escort he was painting nude at the time, usually exaggerating the genitalia as he had Rebecca's mouth.

Over the years it developed that the painting was especially cruel because her mouth seemed to promise something Rebecca did not deliver, a kind of louche attitude that drew men to her when her face was in repose. It made you attend to her lips, and her lips made you attend to what her lips might do. In this way she had been importuned by a number of imaginative men in the two decades since her divorce—although not before it, when she was inclined to keep her lower lip tucked under the upper in a gesture that was characteristic of her youth. She had spent about a year halfheartedly seeing an intellectual property lawyer, who in his insistence on talking only about himself finally reminded her so much of a cut-rate Peter that she had simply stopped re-turning his calls and messages. She and another photographer with whom she had always had an easy friendship became a couple for a while, but then he moved to San Francisco and mar-ried a nice Chinese woman young enough to give him children. She had broken the heart of a short story writer to whom Doro-thea had introduced her; he was good-looking, in an odd and arresting way, and smart, too, but he was crazy about her, even talked about moving in together. This made her both suspicious and claustrophobic, and after a while he just gave up. "You're making a terrible mistake," he told her, and in the abstract she thought he was probably right.

She was bad at breaking up with people once she got involved, and so now she was less and less likely to get involved. It was always so difficult to put into words exactly what was wrong without sounding mean or trivial. She remembered one evening so vividly that she could see the food in front of her—rosy tuna tartare, with some elaborate radish decoration around the rim of the white plate—and a handsomish man who had begun a long disquisition on the German character, on how there was a certain order and linear thinking that prefigured so much that had happened in literature, music, and of course world affairs. And as he raised his fork and said, "The rise of fascism was inevitable," she had heard a sort of click in her head that said, "No. Absolutely not."

"May I come up?" he'd said nicely as the doorman pretended not to eavesdrop.

"No," Rebecca replied. "But thank you for dinner."

That was her last date. Unless you counted sharing coffee from a thermos in a tree stand at dawn and eating a nine-hundred-calorie grilled cheese sandwich. Which she most certainly did not. That thought had not seriously crossed her mind, nor the suspicion that every time Jim Bates looked at her lower lip he had an impulse to take it gingerly between his front teeth. She had seen him flush more than once in the tree stand, and had wondered a little, then finally concluded that because of his fair complexion he was especially sensitive to changes in temperature. But actually he was especially sensitive to Rebecca Winter's lower lip. Luckily she hadn't a clue. Like the deer, you had to sneak up slowly on Rebecca or else she would bolt. Considering her marriage, that wasn't surprising.

A WOMAN WITHOUT A MAN

From *The New York Times* Society section, October 2, 1980:

Rebecca Grace Winter, the daughter of Mr. and Mrs. Oscar Winter of Manhattan, was married at her parents' home yesterday to Peter Soames Symington, son of Richard and the late Rachel Symington of Oxford, England.

The bride is a graduate of Mount Holyoke College and the Art Students League, where she holds a certificate in painting. Her father is the president of Freeman Foundations, a manufacturer of women's undergarments, which was founded by the bride's maternal grandfather.

Professor Symington graduated from the University of Cambridge and has a doctorate in comparative literature from Harvard. He is a professor of English literature at Columbia University and is the author of "Medieval Iconography and the Body Triumphant," published by W. W. Norton & Company. His father was vice-master at Balliol College, Oxford. His previous marriage ended in divorce.

FISH, BICYCLE

The last time Rebecca had seen her former husband was at Ben's college graduation. She was delighted to see that he was losing his hair, especially in the rear crown, so that what he had left in the front looked like an afterthought. Of course Peter was easing up on seventy, an age when a man might be forgiven follicular failure. But Rebecca forgave him nothing. She told herself that this was not because he had betrayed her but because he had betrayed his son. It was one of those statements that sounded sensible until you compared it against actual human psychology.

"I don't know why you have such a hard time admitting that you are just plain pissed," Dorothea said.

"The man didn't deserve you, sweetheart!" said her father.

"I always liked Peter," her mother said.

The minuet of their marriage was, in memory, mortifying to her: Peter would do something—miss dinner, make a slighting comment or a mess—and she would gather up her shreds of dignity and respond with the silent treatment. Except that Peter liked the silent treatment—he found it restful. In a rage she would have long imaginary conversations in the shower in which she would confront and unnerve him. Eventually she would try to lure him back, disgusted by her determination to be pleasant at all costs, to avoid conflict. But Peter liked conflict, too, at least the edgy understated intellectual sort. Their relationship was like playing chess except that one person had all the larger pieces and the other—her—a line of sad little pawns. Check check check. Checkmate.

All that meant that she had forgotten how much she had actually enjoyed being married in the beginning. When the stratum of her earth had rearranged itself, after the dust storms of Ben's infancy and childhood, the tornadoes of her marital upheavals, and the tsunami of their divorce, it had covered over forever the memory of the way he had once run his long fingers, with their savagely bitten nails, up the insides of her legs and around her pelvis until her eyes lost all focus and she gasped helplessly. She had lost all memory of how they had lain on the long uncomfortable settee on Sunday mornings talking about what was in the *Times*. Or, more often, Rebecca listening while Peter talked. Sometimes Peter was in the paper, a review, a quotation, and she would read aloud while he repeated, "Oh, come now. Come now, Becky Sharp," as though it was just all too much, being significant, being revered. When Peter was in the *Times* they almost always had a long afternoon of inventive sex. It never occurred to Rebecca to wonder how Peter would respond to seeing her name in the *Times*.

That was later.

Eventually it turned out that Becky Sharp was Becky Dull, her knees and thighs familiar country. The biggest difference between the two of them was in fact the biggest difference there could be between two people. Rebecca disliked change, and Peter lived for it. It was why he was such a successful academic. Every September, every January, a brightly patterned carpet of upturned faces would materialize in his seminar room or lecture hall, and he would set out to win them over. Deft seduction was his most conspicuous character trait.

Rebecca had met him at a dinner party; the guest who was meant to sit to his right had broken an ankle falling down the escalator at Saks, and Rebecca had been recruited in her stead. On the way down to the street in the small mahogany-faced elevator she had been so focused on what she imagined was Peter's breath on the nape of her neck—which was, in fact, Peter's breath on the nape of her neck, a technique that he found had never let him down—that she failed to move when the doors slid open to the rococo lobby, and as Peter stepped forward he had been pressed against the back of her. That was part of the technique, too.

That Saturday he took her to lunch in Little Italy. Naturally, he spoke Italian. He was, at the time, still married, although only nominally, he said. She would learn that Peter was always more or less nominally married. But that was later, too.

Rebecca had little experience with men, although she was nearly thirty. A nice high school boyfriend who was a truly terrible kisser. A number of brief entanglements in college. An art school lover she would run into at an opening a decade after, only to discover what she ought to have suspected, that he preferred men.

Her junior year she had spent a semester in Florence, but she had heard so many warnings about Italian men—"So much for Catholic morality!" her mother had cried at the end of one sermonette, as Sonya snorted like an angry bull—that if one so much as smiled absently at her in a trattoria she chugged her double espresso and fled. Her biography had all the trappings of sophistication but no actual sophistication at all.

Otherwise she would have realized that some of Peter's technique was a little shopworn. Otherwise, when he sent his first wife and their two young children back to England in first-family exile and persuaded the university to shift him from one apartment building to another, with better views and light, so he and Rebecca could start afresh, she would have seen the inevitable shape of her own future.

"He didn't break the glass," said Rebecca's grandmother on her wedding day, sitting in a corner of the entrance hall in a floral dress that smelled of camphor.

"Oh, for goodness' sake," Rebecca's mother had whispered.

Her grandmother's distress that Peter had not smashed the traditional glass underfoot at the end of the ceremony, that there had been no chuppah and no rabbi, had been muted somewhat by the wedding announcement. "You don't know what a big deal it is for a Jew to get one of these things in *The New York Times*," her grandmother had said in a loud whisper. Rebecca's mother was miffed that the paper, after doing a bit of investigating, had refused to describe her as a concert pianist, or even as a pianist at all. Peter had looked at the misty photograph of Rebecca and read the copy below and said, his accent sharp as a paper cut, "And so we mark the first time that the words 'Balliol College' and 'women's undergarments' have appeared in print in tandem."

There are two kinds of men: men who want a wife who is predictable, and men who want a wife who is exotic. For some reason, Peter had thought she was the latter. But even if that had been the case, the problem inherent remains the same—once she becomes a wife, the exotic becomes familiar, and thus predictable, and thus not what was wanted at all. Those few women who stayed exotic usually were considered, after a few years, to be crazy.

Rebecca learned this over time, and to her sorrow. As with many marriages, hers was based on essential misconceptions. In her case she had been misled into thinking Peter was reliable, perhaps because he was very careful always to put cedar shoe trees into his shoes and because he always wore the same cologne, a bay rum that could be had only from a shop in a London arcade.

It turned out that he was not reliable, just finicky about small personal things like that. He still used a shaving brush and a straight razor.

But Rebecca had liked being married to him for a long time, or at least had liked being part of a pair, having someone to talk to even if he did not seem to be listening, having someone to warm the bed beneath the duvet on cold nights when the old radiators knocked more than they burned. She liked taking an arm on a slick street, having someone pay for the cab. Perhaps she used the words "my husband" more often than many women. She liked reading his manuscripts and didn't much mind that he was not as delighted by the paintings she produced. She was not delighted by them much, either. They had a flat, lifeless quality. It was not until one of her professors told her the photographs she was taking as the basis for some of her paintings were much more interesting than the paintings themselves that she had shifted permanently from painting to photography and found her calling.

Perhaps that was the beginning of the end. Or maybe it was the baby. Or maybe it was simple numerology. At thirty he had married his first wife. At forty he had married Rebecca. At fifty he married the assistant curator with whom Rebecca had surprised him in the back bedroom at a cocktail party farewell for a university colleague. They were in the room with the coats piled on the bed, so they certainly meant to get caught. When Rebecca arrived home Peter refused her demand that he sleep on the couch in his study. "I have a perfectly fine bed in which I intend to sleep," he said, unbuttoning his shirt and releasing a whiff of secondhand Diorissimo, and sex.

So Rebecca had slept on the couch instead. "Mommy," Ben had said sternly next morning, "you're in the wrong place for you."

Sometimes she thought it was not losing her husband she had minded most, but losing the lovely big apartment they'd shared, with its windowed kitchen and its herringbone floors. The university's apartment, into which the assistant curator would move, and where she would eventually raise their twin daughters after giving up her job. Bad move, Rebecca had thought, assuming, correctly, that in the foreseeable future the curator would need to support herself once more.

"I like my old room better," Ben had said when he and Rebecca moved into the place on West Seventy-Sixth Street. The curator wife had called him Benjie, until her own children were born, when she began calling him "your son" and his bed had been moved to the smallest bedroom so the twins could have a larger one. Until then Rebecca had occasionally thought of warning the woman of what would happen when Peter turned sixty. Which did happen when Peter turned sixty. The new woman was a graduate student whose name was Piper. The twins, according to Ben, were acting out because of abandonment. Peter was unchanged.

"I thought you'd seen this coming," Peter had said the night Rebecca had surprised him with the soon-to-be third Mrs. Symington.

She hadn't. Sometimes now she was still amazed, and mortified, that she hadn't. Peter liked stories, liked reading them, telling them, analyzing them. Beginning, middle, end. Drama. Rebecca simply wasn't much of a story. If it hadn't been for the Kitchen Counter series she wouldn't have been a story at all. It was only in the last few years that she had begun to realize that this wasn't her fault. She realized that marriage doesn't really make much of a story. Even in a marriage as truncated as her own—nine years, more or less—most of it is the mundane middle part. That was the part Peter couldn't bear. That was the part Rebecca had liked most. It was the part she still missed, missed terribly without even knowing it.

ONE TURKEY AFTER
ANOTHER

Bebe hired a black woman who lived in Harlem to cook dinner
for her husband, her six-year-old daughter, her parents, and a
couple who lived in the apartment above. There was a twenty-
four-pound turkey, corn bread dressing, mashed sweet potatoes
with marshmallows, and three kinds of pie. Bebe refused to tip
the woman because she arrived nearly forty minutes late to the
apartment. The next day, eating a turkey sandwich with salt and
mayonnaise, Rebecca decided Thanksgiving was the best holiday, although she had little to choose from: her family never cel-
ebrated Hanukkah but her father was militant about ignoring
Christmas and insisted they spend December 25 eating Chinese
takeout and going to the movies.

Rebecca liked moo shu beef but liked turkey sandwiches better.

THANKSGIVING 1966

Bebe decided to try Thanksgiving at the Berkshire Hotel. From then on, Winter family Thanksgivings were held at the Berkshire. However, by the time Rebecca was married and concerned about how to explain that she and Peter did not want a hotel meal on a holiday, her parents had decided to go to Delray Beach from November to March.

The Delray Beach and Tennis Club had a Thanksgiving buffet. Rebecca did not visit her parents in Florida until December. Peter did not visit them at all.

"It's not my holiday, darling," Peter said when she expressed relief that they could have their own Thanksgiving meal, in their own home. He said this every Thanksgiving at some point. He said the Pilgrims ate turkey because their religion forbade joy. The American guests all laughed, secretly impressed by the use of the archaic past tense of *forbid*. One year a historian became contentious: "Now, you see, that's a basic bowdlerization of the Puritan experience in America," he said with his mouth full. "Oh, dear Lord, Owen, next you'll provide us with a history of the yam in an agrarian culture," Peter drawled, and everyone laughed again.

THANKSGIVING 1990

Rebecca and Ben had Thanksgiving dinner at the Delray Beach and Tennis Club. "This is like a restaurant," said Ben, who was six. "He misses his father," said Rebecca's father, making a well in his potatoes for his gravy. "Look, Benjie, do it like this."

"This is my daughter," said Bebe to one of her friends who stopped by the table.

"The famous photographer?" the woman said.

"She's getting a divorce," Bebe said.

THANKSGIVING 2010

"Anyone can prepare a turkey," it said in one of Rebecca's cookbooks, still sitting on the shelf above the refrigerator in her apartment in New York. She groaned, and not simply because she imagined she could hear Ben, on the inflatable mattress in the cottage's second bedroom, having sex with the young woman he has brought up to visit with him.

(In fact Ben was doing push-ups. Rebecca is unable to tell the difference between the breathing of a man performing rhythmic exercise and one in the throes of coitus. Which may be the clearest reflection of her sex life during her marriage. Peter Symington was a thrilling and imaginative lover before the clinking of champagne glasses at the wedding lunch; after, he was burning calories and fantasizing about the girl in the short skirt in the front row of his survey course. While Ben does push-ups, Ben's girlfriend, a young woman named Amanda, has gone outside to have a cigarette. This habit will eventually, nominally, lead to the end of her relationship with Ben at a New Year's Eve party. That, and the following conversation between Rebecca and her son over Thanksgiving dinner:

"So then he shot the raccoon."

"He shot him? He couldn't trap him and take him somewhere else?"

"Apparently if you do that they come right back. He's something of a wildlife specialist and he was convinced that the raccoon would be back in the attic within a day or two if it wasn't killed."

To which Amanda said sadly, "I can't imagine any circumstances under which it's necessary to kill an animal."

Rebecca has become accustomed to the speed with which her son's romantic relationships begin, blossom, and then blow apart, like a time-lapse photograph of a claymore landing in a rose garden. She also knows that hearing the sort of sentence that admits to no possible alternative to a set scenario is, to Ben, like being force-fed adrenaline. She can almost see the pressure increase in the blue vein in his slender throat.

"Wait, you're saying there's no circumstance under which you'd shoot an animal? Like a grizzly bear attacking in Yellowstone?"

Perhaps because his father believed in the Socratic method of child rearing—"Tell us, Ben, what precisely is it about rap music that you find particularly compelling?"—Ben has become an indefatigable arguer. It is on New Year's Eve, when a rat crosses their path on Avenue A and Ben mutters, "Under no circumstances could I hurt that animal," that Amanda had had enough.

"She just wasn't smart enough," Ben would tell Rebecca on the phone. "And she smoked. Her mouth tasted like an ashtray."

But that was later.)

Rebecca groaned at the thought of her tenants opening the

holiday cookbook, or any of the other cookbooks that were rel-
ics from her marriage, with their India ink marginalia: "P. didn't
like"; "P. hated"; the blessed, very rare, "P. liked." Only boeuf
bourguignon, which took her all day, with those endless pearl
onions to blanch, score, peel, has the legend "P. loved!" The
memory of that exclamation point is a mortification. So, too, is
the fact that this morning she realized she had violated one of
the basic tenets of any competent cook: she had purchased a
turkey without comparing its size to the size of her oven. For
fifteen minutes she sat at the table, staring at the bird, greasy
with butter, caped in cheesecloth, as though it might shrink.

"No way," Ben had said as she held the roasting pan in front
of the oven door and angled it this way and that.

And an hour later, "Wow, Mom, you totally lucked out."

That was after she had sent him and the turkey to Tea for
Two, the only place in town she could imagine that had both a
large oven and no turkey inside it. "Sarah—man, can she talk!—
Sarah says she'll send someone over with it around five."

"What a sweet thing," Amanda had said.

"You didn't have to listen to her," said Ben.

(Later Amanda would remember this as one of the moments
when she fell a little out of love with him. Also when he ate the
last piece of pumpkin pie for Sunday breakfast and then went
running alone without asking if she wanted to come.)

The potatoes were waiting to be mashed, the string beans
steaming, and deep dark sliding up the side of the mountain
when there was a tentative knock at the front door. When Rebecca opened it a middle-aged man with melancholy eyes and
pouchy cheeks stood holding a large cardboard box.

"It is I, Ms. Winter, bearing the bird." It was the phrasing as
much as the voice that made her recognize Tad.

"I'm so sorry, Mr. Brinks. I've never seen you without your
makeup." At the self-serve gas station pumps, going into the
pharmacy, several times at Tea for Two—but never with this fair

baby skin and slightly flattened pug nose. Rebecca reached for the box.

"Oh, certainly not. This is both hot and heavy, so to speak, and I would be remiss if I did not bring it in." Ben appeared behind his mother. "Oh, goodness, I'm interrupting the festivities. Perhaps this young man will take it so I can be on my way."

"Would you like to join us for dinner? It's an enormous turkey, as I'm sure you can tell. Ben, take that from him. It's really far too large for three people. I can't imagine what I was thinking." Living in the past, Rebecca thought, when the long pine table in the dining room was crowded with friends. Ah, well. She had learned to live without them, it seemed.

"This is turkey enough for twelve," Ben said.

"It's a lovely thought, but I will be breaking bread with my mother and my aunt Ruth. I merely stopped at Sarah's for corn muffins and she asked me if I would bring the bird to you."

"Corn bread stuffing?" Amanda said brightly.

"Stuffing is a breeding ground for bacteria," Tad said solemnly. "Stuffing a turkey is as dangerous as botulism."

"Here comes a slow painful death!" Ben cried when he shoveled in a forkful of stuffing an hour later. The turkey was perfectly done, and Sarah had sent a thermos of gravy that she'd made herself from the pan drippings and some tawny port.

"There are some lovely people here," Rebecca said.

"That guy wears makeup?"

"He's a clown. A professional clown. The Magnificent Mo Mo."

The week before in Tea for Two, Tad had joined her for coffee and Rebecca had asked him how he'd chosen his profession. "I purchased a kit," he said. She'd thought he'd misunderstood her, but according to Tad someone, somewhere, offered by mail a beginner's clown kit: makeup, wig, an instruction manual on how to make balloon animals. Rebecca had thought of asking to photograph some of the balloon animals, but in her experience people only wanted you to photograph *them*. And even she had to admit that balloon animals in black-and-white instead of color would lose a great deal of their balloon animalness.

"None of it is of the highest quality," Tad had added, "but it got me started."

"Had you always wanted to—" Rebecca hesitated. Was it possible to use the word *clown* as a verb?

Tad had interrupted her. "I was interested in entertaining," he said solemnly. "Being a clown was collateral."

Rebecca thought of the story of the Rothrock competition. The man had wanted to be an operatic singer and had settled for balloon animals.

"I had a similar experience," she said.

"Oh, no," Tad said. "You were born to be a great photographer."

"I'm not sure anyone is born to be anything," Rebecca had replied.

"Remember Nicholas Lindstrom at my birthday party, locking himself in the bathroom because of the clown?" Ben said, peeling a piece of skin off the turkey breast.

"I think of it every time I see Tad. He's so earnest about his— is *clowning* a word?—that I'd never dare mention it."

"When I was a little girl there was a clown at every single party," said Amanda, who had grown up on Park Avenue. (Strike two with Ben.)

"That work on the wall of the room we're using is really good," said Ben. "The crosses? Really really good. I keep wondering what's underneath."

"Underneath what?"

"The crosses. They're little graves, right? What's in the graves? Baby birds? Kittens?"

"What a terrible thought," said Amanda, putting her fork down.

"That's interesting," Rebecca said. "I've thought about them quite a lot, but it's never occurred to me that there's anything beneath them. The earth doesn't look disturbed. Take a good look. I don't think there's been any digging."

"Are they like those memorial things that you see sometimes on the road?"

"I had the same thought, but these are out in the middle of nowhere. They obviously can't involve a car accident, and I have to assume there are too many of them to commemorate a single event. Or perhaps not. I just don't know."

"And you haven't moved them to get a better look?" Ben waved his knife at Rebecca. "I know, I know, how many times have I heard it: if you manipulate the scene you distort the image. In other words, don't . . . move . . . anything. What's there is the point. The Rebecca Winter aesthetic." Ben turned to Amanda. "There exist images of my baby ass that some people genuinely think are sand dunes, or the Sahara."

"Oh, you," said Amanda, aiming for playful and succeeding only at sounding puzzled.

"You've been reading too much art criticism," said Rebecca, smiling at her son.

"If you had three or four more of those, you could have a show," Ben said, making a well in the center of his mashed potatoes and filling it with gravy. "You could call it the White Cross series."

"I will if I find any more." Such a jolt she had felt, when she'd stepped off a deer trail beneath a lanky old pine and had seen another white cross leaning against its trunk. Beneath it was one of those plaster casts of a handprint that kindergarten teachers must learn in Education 101. Rebecca had made one like it herself for some long-ago Mother's Day, but she was quite certain that after the statutory time limit—a year? a month?—Bebe would have asked Sonya to dispose of it. Only the items she gave her father were safe, ranged along a shelf in his office that, for some reason, also held a burgundy leather set of the *Encyclo-*

paedia Britannica: an ashtray painted blue and white, a mosaic tray from day camp made out of shards of old dishes, later some small paintings of a Sabrett cart on a corner and the Empire State Building spire stabbing an unlikely collection of cumulus clouds. Her father had mourned her career as a painter. He never said so, but she could tell that he thought photography was a second-rate artistic pursuit.

"I went to see Pop Pop last week," said Ben around a mouthful of stuffing.

"How was he?"

"Good. He's always good. We watched the news and the Giants game. Sonya made us some kind of goulash." Sonya may have once been a good cook, but decades of making food for the Winter family had flattened any formerly sharp edges of her cuisine. Rebecca's mother was fond of what Peter had called "Presbyterian meals": chicken à la king, tomato juice, and oyster crackers. "As an Englishman, I feel perfectly at home with the food served in your parents' home, darling," he had said when he was still in his early charming phase, before Rebecca realized that *darling* was a British social convention and not an endearment, and that it was frequently used to mean its opposite.

"Did you go to see Nana, too?" Rebecca said.

"Nah. I mean, what's the point? She thinks I'm the guy who's there to mop the floor. Or she doesn't even notice because she's playing the piano."

"Your grandmother plays the piano?" said Amanda. The poor girl, her sentences dropped like stones into the pond of their conversation, fell to the bottom and disappeared. Rebecca blamed her son. For some reason he always picked women he would find easy to discard.

"Endlessly," Ben said.

Bebe had never noticed much of anything while she was playing the piano. Rebecca had sometimes thought she could have walked into the apartment with some boy, taken him back to her room, had loud sex with him, and shown him the door naked, and her mother would have continued with the second movement of the *Pathétique* Sonata. If there had been such a boy. If she had been such a girl. Instead she did her algebra or American history as the plaster and lath of her bedroom walls hummed.

"My mother has dementia," Rebecca said to Amanda. "We don't know exactly what she sees or knows."

"Really, Mom? Really?"

"Didn't Pop Pop ask if you'd seen her?"

"Sure. I said I had. I said she was asking for him." Rebecca can almost hear Sonya's grunt as he says it. Ben is like his father; he can lie fluently, but unlike his father he almost always does it in a good cause. He does not lie to these young women when he leaves them. He tells them the truth, unsparingly. Which she supposes is also a bit like his father.

"This is such good pie," Amanda says later. "Can I have your recipe?" Ah, the girlfriends. So transparent. And of course Rebecca had been a girlfriend once, too, telling Peter's stepmother that she hoped to learn how to make summer pudding. "Perhaps our housekeeper can help you with that," the woman had said. Frosty, it had been, and at the time Rebecca had put it down to being English, later to the fact that Peter's stepmother apparently had never prepared so much as a cup of tea, later still to the idea that Rebecca was the second wife and perhaps Peter's family had quite liked the first one. Or did now that the first wife was wife no longer.

"It's the recipe on the pie filling can," said Rebecca, who already sensed she would not be seeing Amanda again.

"It's great," Ben said, and he put his arm around Rebecca's shoulder and kissed the top of her head. "Everything was great. As always."

LEFTOVER TURKEY

"Can I offer you some leftover turkey?" Rebecca said on Saturday as Jim Bates pulled his truck up her driveway.

"That's really nice of you to offer," he said. "But here's the deal if you're a single guy. Every woman in town offers you leftover turkey. It's turkey fest. Plus, one word: Sarah."

"A tray of leftovers?"

"An entire turkey."

"She made you an entire turkey?"

He nodded.

"That's extremely thoughtful."

"A twenty-two-pound turkey."

Rebecca began to laugh and, in a minute, so did he. Each fed upon the other, until the stuffy cab of the truck, which smelled of tar, glue, and peanut butter, filled with the sound of their laughter. It was somewhat excessive for the situation.

"Extremely, extremely thoughtful," Rebecca said, climbing out of the cab of the truck and taking her cameras from the back.

"I don't even really like turkey that much," he said, and they both began to laugh again.

It had been a good morning's work. The light was clear and strong despite the cover of the trees, and the big birds, perhaps in response to the cool temperatures, had flown to and fro above them, sometimes dipping and wheeling lower and lower until it almost seemed that they were posing. Jim Bates had squinted at the screen of Rebecca's camera, looking at a photograph of one of the bald eagles in flight. "That's a beauty," he said, and she wasn't certain if he meant the photograph or the bird, or both.

"Same time tomorrow?" he said as she headed toward the cottage.

"One of us should bring turkey sandwiches," Rebecca said.

"I shouldn't have said that about Sarah," he said. "She's a nice woman. She made a whole lot of turkeys, a couple for the church, one for me. I'm my own soup kitchen, I guess."

"She cooked ours as well. It was too large for the oven here."

"That's a vintage stove you're working with. And it's electric. Really sad."

"I regret ever making that remark. You will never let me forget it."

"Tragic," Jim Bates said.

Ben was at the window when she went inside. She put her camera bag on the dining room table.

"Who was that?" Ben said.

"The man I work with. He's a roofer."

"You work with a roofer?"

"He also tracks birds for the state wildlife authorities. I'm taking photographs of the birds for them."

Ben put down a sandwich he was holding. Rebecca couldn't help noticing that it was a turkey sandwich.

"You're taking bird photographs for the state?"

"Why not? It's a public service." She knew she was making it sound like the pro bono work she had done from time to time for charities in the city and tried not to dwell on the $400 check she had received the week before, or how overjoyed she had been to see the telltale envelope with the transparent window.

"So if you take the photographs what does he do?"

"He tracks the birds with a device that reads their tags. When we find one that hasn't been tagged, he makes a note of it."

"And he's a roofer?"

"He is the roofer who took care of the raccoon that was living in the house when I first arrived here."

Amanda came in from the bedroom, gathering her tawny hair into a clip. She was wearing workout clothes. She had invited Rebecca to join her in an hour of yoga, but Rebecca had demurred.

"I'm sorry, but I still can't understand why he had to shoot the raccoon," she said, and this time Ben rolled his eyes. "Make fun of me if you want," Amanda said, draping herself across his shoulders. "I still think it's barbaric."

"He's a big guy," said Ben.

"I got some very good photographs today."

"You should have brought him in."

"It's just a job, Benjamin."

"Don't go all Lady Chatterley on me, Mom," Ben said, disentangling himself.

"Benjamin!"

"Just saying. Just saying."

"I know I should understand the allusion, but I was an art history major," said Amanda.

"There's no need," said Rebecca, narrowing her eyes and scowling at Ben.

"Did I hit a nerve?" Ben said.

"Is there enough turkey for a sandwich?" Amanda said, and almost despite herself Rebecca started to laugh. "Pay no attention to me," she said when both Ben and Amanda looked at her. "I'll have one, too."

THE DOG RETURNS,
AND STAYS

The dog came back on Monday. Rebecca was feeling down-hearted. She hated to see Ben go, and she always liked to send him on his way with a check. But as he and Amanda loaded the car on Sunday afternoon he had waved her off. "Pop Pop gave me money," Ben said, and what could she say? That she knew her father was stuck in 1958, that his idea of a munificent gift was a crisp twenty-dollar bill? She wished she had a couple of crisp twenties to keep the singles in her wallet company. "Your mother's made of money," her father likes to tell her son. "That's why she gave up her painting for those pictures she takes, for the money. The dinero. The shekels. The mean green."

"They're photographs, Pop Pop," Ben says. "Not pictures."

"Same difference!" her father always says.

At dawn she threw the sheets from the guest bedroom into the ancient washing machine and left it to sashay across the basement floor making a clatter. Even down there, with the thick stone walls muffling the outdoor sounds, she could hear the gunshots from the hunters in the surrounding woods. She had almost forgotten the start of hunting season. She didn't know how long it would go on, what the rules were. Jim Bates would have told her, but he had a way of talking about things, assuming she already understood them, that was flattering but made it hard to ask questions without feeling foolish.

She knew exactly what a gunshot sounded like now. She knew that it was more than a sound, that it was like thunder or a breaking glass, something you felt inside. The owner of the cottage had had signs posted forbidding hunting on his land, but the years, and the rains, and the seasons had dried, curled, and obliterated them. Each time there was a gunshot she flinched.

"You're gonna want this," Jim Bates had told her when he gave her a big orange vest. "But I'd stay close to home for the first few days. Only the smart guys hang in past Wednesday, and the smart guys know to stay far away from anybody's house."

She was bound and determined to go about her business as though bullets weren't whizzing through the trees, but on Monday morning, the first morning, when the shooting was fiercest, she hadn't had to go far at all. As though in response to her son's wishes she found another cross right away, on the slope not far from the house, and she imagined someone putting it there, and it made her a little afraid. She thought of Ben and Amanda in the back room, of the late lunch at the dining table, of the dishes being washed in the sink after they were gone, Rebecca's face a little slack and sad, and she could see it all from the outside looking in, the way an eavesdropper would have seen it, the way the person who put the cross there might have. There was no disturbance to the earth, only what seemed to be a deep pillow of leaves, the curling brown remains of this year atop last year and the year before. In the beginning, the soft moss and spongy earth had made her feel as though the ground was porous, unreliable, even alive somehow, but now she was accustomed to it, like breaking in a new pair of shoes, accustomed to the soft snapping sounds of the branches overhead that caught even the softest breezes, and the occasional crash of a deer nearby frightened into haste. Those sounds were her sounds now, embedded inside her so that she did not startle and scarcely noticed. But still she shivered at the idea that someone had been this close to the house, perhaps watching her standing alone, etched black by the lamplight.

The cross was accompanied by a baby doll in a limp pink dress. Her hair had been shampooed, so that the careful coif of the manufacturer had become a kind of snarled yellow mess. She looked like every doll every little girl had ever ruined while giving her a bath. Rebecca had had one herself. Hanging on the cross was what looked like a doll locket, a heart no bigger than the nail on a pinkie toe. Before she even raised the camera Rebecca knew these pictures would be memorable. The doll was sitting up and staring blankly, its plastic legs akimbo. She photographed it, the orange vest rustling around her.

Around four every day now she found herself desperate for a nap. Her vision blurred, her mind did, too, as she tried to reread *Buddenbrooks* and *Middlemarch*. But she was terrified at the idea of becoming that person, dozing away the afternoon. She usually forced herself to go out again, to bracket her day with hikes, as though she could outwalk her thoughts. The mornings were fine but the late afternoons not so, the light dulled and dimming early. She felt some strange yearning, but she couldn't decide what it was for. Not for the city: it seemed like another country to her now, remembered, not felt. She knew if she were there, walking past the market with its glistening stacks of fruit that sometimes rolled onto the pavement, stepping into the pharmacy for overpriced shampoo and body cream, passing windows full of nice clothes like the clothes she already has (once she got a linen blouse home only to discover that she owned one almost exactly like it), she would be convinced that she could no longer stand to be away, that she missed it all terribly. But from here that life seemed unreal, like something she saw in a movie. She wondered if that's how her grandparents had managed to leave the old country behind, whether it had ceased to exist as a discernible thing once it was gone along the watery horizon, whether they had told themselves that someday they would come back to reclaim it.

She'd been amazed to discover after a while that that was how she felt about Peter, the divorce, not pain but simple dislocation. Her marriage had been like a new silk dress, so beautiful and undulating, except that after a while the edges of the sleeves gray, there is a spot of wine, the hem drags. If her love affair with Peter had stopped after six months it would have been a gorgeous memorable thing. But in love no one ever leaves well enough alone, and so it settles into a strange unsatisfactory kind of friendship or sours into mutual recriminations and regret, the dress pushed to the back of the closet, limp and so unnew, embalmed in plastic because of what it once was.

The night threw itself over the day fast now, sucked the light in and distilled it to one silvery spot in the sky where the moon hung. Sometimes she found herself hiking back to the cabin in near dark. The only spot of light was the white flag rippling from the roof where Jim Bates had put it up, and the faint glow from deep inside where she left a rickety floor lamp on in the bedroom. It made the day go by, staying on the move, but on the first day of hunting season she knew it wasn't safe. In the graying day her orange vest had been dampened to an earth tone, not bright enough to make it easy to pick her out from between the trees.

The dog was on the back steps, his head between his paws. When she saw him her eyes narrowed. The shooting had stopped, and it was silent all around her except for the slapping sound of his long tail against the siding.

"This is not where you live," she said.

He stood.

"Go home," she said.

He sat and looked attentive.

"I don't care for dogs," she said.

He cocked his head as though he was thinking either, no problem, neither have any of the other people I've lived with, or, liar. He settled on the second, stepped forward and sniffed her hand, then licked it and lay down at her feet.

"You can't come in the house," she said, opening the door, thinking of all the leftover turkey in the refrigerator.

"I think I've got a dog," she said later that week when she called Ben from the service station as she put gas in her car, watching nervously as the total clicked higher and higher.

"You're allergic," Ben said.

"That's your father."

"I don't know about that. The new wife has a dog. A spaniel, I think. Or maybe it's not a spaniel. Maybe it's one of those hypoallergenic dogs. Did you want a dog?"

"No. He just appeared. He's good company."

"That's good. You could use a little company." Occasionally Rebecca wished her son would not be so very kind to her, as though she was the losing pitcher on a Little League team. She hoped it wasn't some unconscious retaliation for that, or for his comments about photographing birds, or helping Jim Bates, that made her say, "Amanda seems nice."

"Whatever, Mom," Ben replied.

SITTING IN A TREE, AGAIN

Three things happened at the beginning of December.

The building in which Rebecca lived in New York announced a maintenance increase of 10 percent to replace the roof. (1540)

The nursing home where her mother lived announced an adjustment in monthly charges based on higher costs of fuel oil and staff salaries. (2210)

She ran out of firewood.

Oddly enough, that last seemed the worst, or at least the most real. It reminded her of the time after she had been served with divorce papers and been told Peter wanted a swift resolution in time for a June wedding, his fiancée being four months pregnant—and was it actually semantically possible, she had wondered, to have a wife and a fiancée at the same time if you were not an adherent of one of the hinkier Mormon sects? It so happened that on her way to throw open her door to the dishy Latino process server, she had hit her foot on the stone obelisk which she used as a doorstop—and which, she realized later, she had purchased on her honeymoon, Peter saying, "That is precisely the sort of item that holds you up in customs"—and broken her toe. For a week afterward she had been obsessed with her toe, finding shoes that would not worry it, taping it with clear surgical tape, tracking the slow progression of its color, like a sunset in reverse, from black to purple to yellowy mauve. Her toe stopped her from thinking too much about her future. The firewood did the same for her finances.

She bought three cords of wood from a man who sold firewood from a truck at the side of the gas station; she knew it wouldn't last long but she wasn't carrying the cash for more, and the man had snorted when she asked if he accepted credit cards. When Jim Bates came to pick her up the Saturday morning after and saw the wood stacked by the front door, he all at once looked like the kind of guy you wouldn't want to cross in a bar.

"You buy this from Kevin?" he said.

"I bought it at the filling station. Why?"

"Don't buy any firewood. It's lying all over these woods, just waiting to be split. I've got a log splitter. I can take care of it."

"Kevin, Sarah's husband?" she said.

"Yeah, never mind, I'll take care of it," he said, climbing into the cab of his truck.

The coffee was so sweet this morning that it tasted like melted coffee ice cream, but she needed the warmth up in the tree stand. Heat rises; maybe cold does, too. Rebecca leaned over the big thermos lid so that the steam wreathed her face. Her nose remained numb. Leaning back against the tree trunk, she could feel the bark even through the down parka, the sweater, the long underwear. The long underwear was her Christmas present to herself. The Greifers, the blessed Greifers, who were always first to buy her work, had decided to acquire one of the photographs of the stone wall, although not one of the bigger ones. She suddenly had three hundred dollars in her wallet and ten times that in her bank account, and had started to think about moving back into her apartment after she finished the term at Carnegie Mellon. Thrilled and delighted, that's what they were at Carnegie Mellon, although still unwilling to increase the stipend. She could tell by the jocular tone of the department chairman's messages that he was thinking she was a warm woman, well-heeled and well-known and nevertheless trying to squeeze more blood from the stone of the fine arts budget.

She had written Ben a check, and gotten real hiking boots. Selling one photograph had given her the illusion of prosperity for a few days. She kept telling herself that it was so much less expensive to live here: she hadn't bought wine since Thanksgiving, and the two dresses she'd brought with her in case of— well, just in case—stood in the corner of her closet like guests who have come to the wrong party and are backing out the door.

And then she had heard about the apartment maintenance, and the nursing home fees, and her week of peace was done. Like those things that have frightened you that are written on your body, struggling in deep water or falling off a high ladder, she now realized that she would never be able to look at her bank statement again without that cold feeling in her chest, an accelerated heartbeat. Years ago some young woman in a blue blazer at her branch had asked if she wanted overdraft coverage, and without thinking she had said, "Why not?" Not long ago she had remembered she had it, and felt exultant for a moment, and then crushed that being able to write checks with no money could be cause for celebration.

"Did you get a deer?" she asked Jim Bates, trying to put money out of her head.

"I got two," he said. "A buck and a doe. A ten-point buck. That's a male deer with ten points on his antlers."

"I had figured that out from context. That's an awful lot of venison for one person."

"I've got as much for you as your freezer will hold."

"I wasn't hinting at that."

"I know. But I give a lot of it away. I've got some nice tenderloins for you, and some chops. And ground venison makes a great chili if you know how to cook."

"I know how to cook."

"There you go."

"I've acquired a dog," she said quietly.

"Did you go to the shelter," Jim Bates asked, "or did you get some fancy breed of dog? I like a Labrador, myself, but even some of those wind up in the shelter. Otherwise you have to pay upwards of a thousand dollars for a Lab puppy."

"He's definitely not a purebred dog," she said.

"Just wondering. I figure most of the people you know have purebred dogs of one kind or another."

For a moment she imagined the cockapoos, dachshunds, and shih tzus of Central Park stumbling through the forest, dried leaves caught in their silky hair, the Yorkshire terriers yapping as they turned in panicked circles: Help! Help! I've just come from the groomer! She tried to hold back a laugh and it emerged as something between a sneeze and a snort.

"Okay, forget it. It's just the way I think of city people with dogs. Plus you're famous. I looked you up. Three million hits."

"Three million," she repeated.

"That's pretty famous."

"I was well-known at one time. I wouldn't say famous. I certainly wouldn't say it any longer. It's difficult to describe. First you have one sort of life and then you have another. I'm sorry, that must sound odd."

"No it doesn't. That's what happens to everybody. You want a cruller?"

Each appreciated this about the other: that they set themselves exclusively to a given task. Photography. Roofing. Bird-watching. Eating. They did not talk while they ate. She ate one cruller, he two. They drank coffee. Neither one was uncomfortable with silence. Jim Bates didn't find this especially notable. Rebecca, having spent her life in New York City, where to sit in the back of a cab without hearing a long list of grievances from either a new immigrant who felt discriminated against or a veteran New Yorker who hated new immigrants, did.

After he'd wiped his fingers on a napkin, Jim said, "Twenty years ago I was in the service in South Carolina. I was married to a girl named Laura." He smiled. "She had blond hair and when she left the room, if I was looking, she'd do this wiggle thing with her butt."

Rebecca had another sip of coffee. She could see her, Laura, wiggling. She could see her wearing blue shorts and a striped tank top. Blondes always wore blue. Rebecca never did.

"Then my father fell off a roof. It was the last thing in the world you'd expect. He'd been running around roofs since he was thirteen, you know. Then this one day he just slid down, fell flat, and died on the spot. I don't know, maybe he didn't fall off the roof. One of the ambulance corps guys said maybe he had a heart attack, or a stroke, and then fell off. Whatever. He died, so I came home. My mother was already gone by then. She got breast cancer. She was the seventh-grade teacher at the middle school. There were a thousand people in the street when she got buried. I don't remember it much, but I remember all those people. She was a good seventh-grade teacher. She was my seventh-grade teacher. That was weird. 'Mr. Bates, can you come up to the board and do problem number three,' that kind of stuff."

"That must have been difficult," Rebecca said.

"I kind of loved it, to tell you the truth. Mr. Bates, and then I'd get home and turn back into Jimmy."

"You loved her."

He picked up the thermos and took a big gulp directly from it, without bothering with the cup lid. Rebecca watched his throat work, up and down, up and down. "Hell, yes," he said, wiping his mouth with his hand, like he had to say and do a manly thing to offset the sentiment.

"She loved you."

"Hell, yes. Well, my mom, you know. It goes with the territory."

"My mother is not that sort of mother."

"Got it," he said. "I had a buddy who had that kind of mother. What about your dad?"

"Better. Good, I suppose. A little odd. Now he's a little vague."

"Yeah, I get that. My father wasn't the sharpest knife, truth be told. I guess she married him because he was big and good-looking, one of those big blond guys, you know."

Rebecca smiled slightly and cocked her head, and Jim Bates turned bright red. That look was one of the single most flirtatious things she had ever done in all the sixty years of her existence, and she hadn't even meant to do it.

He flushed so that it looked as though his face had turned into a night-light. Rebecca found herself flushing, too. "What about yours?" he finally asked. "Do they get along? They still married?"

"Oh yes. They are still married. Until death do us part. Their marriage remains a mystery to me. But it was probably mysterious to them as well. Perhaps all marriage is." Rebecca shrugged. "I don't have much patience with how we all harp on our families."

"It's the most important thing there is," he said flatly. "There's not a day goes by that I don't think of my mother. My dad, too, but different—you know, more business, how he'd handle an overhang, whether he'd do the gutters a different way, that kind of thing. You have brothers? Sisters?"

"Neither."

"Really?"

"And you?"

"I had a brother named Jack. He died of meningitis when he was seven. He was two years older than me. I have a sister who's eight years younger. Her name's Polly."

"That's a lovely old-fashioned name."

"Her real name's Priscilla. She wasn't having that, once she got to first grade. She changed it herself. Our mom said she could do it as long as she kept the *P*. I think my mother was worried she'd name herself Nicole or Danielle or something."

"Do you see her often?"

"Every day."

Rebecca can imagine Polly Bates without even trying hard, Polly Bates or whatever her name is now because surely she's married, her light hair a little darker, her pink cheeks a little fuller, two older kids and maybe a toddler keeping her too busy to do more than throw on sweatpants in the morning and pull her hair back into a ponytail. "Here's Uncle Jim," she'll say when he shows up at the end of the workday. "Take them off my hands before I lock them out of the house, Jimmy. Give me five minutes peace."

"Do you like her?" Rebecca said.

He took another cruller from the bag. Light was creeping through the tree canopy, but it was the flat surly light of an over-cast winter day. It seemed to take him a long time to chew. "Yeah," he finally said. "I do." He took a deep breath. "She's had some health issues. Just a whole bunch of stuff, for a long time." The flushed and harried mother in the sweat suit disap-peared; suddenly the children were quieter, more tentative, and she was wearing a head scarf. Breast cancer, Rebecca thought. Men hate to talk about breast cancer. His mother. His sister. She put a hand on his arm without thinking.

"I'm sorry," she said, and he nodded.

She realized that this was the longest conversation she had had with anyone in quite some time. Perhaps the longest conversation she had ever had with a man, unless she counted Ben. She had imagined she would have nice long conversations with Peter after they were married, but it had turned out that marriage in the circles in New York in which they traveled consisted of men who pontificated publicly, and the women who let their faces go still while they did so. Maybe that was true of marriage everywhere. Between times, in their own living rooms, the men seemed to be resting for the next round of pontificating and so saved their strength by staying silent.

A bald eagle flew overhead, circled, and landed on a tree nearby. There was a branch from a big evergreen in Rebecca's way. "That was a bad angle," she said.

"Yeah, but, come on, great moment, right?" He passed her the thermos. She drank directly from it, too. It seemed rude somehow not to.

"Hey, we're getting paid to sit here and talk like this," Jim Bates said. "Don't people like you usually pay someone else to listen to your troubles?"

"I've avoided that particular trap," said Rebecca.

He smiled. "Atta girl," he said.

"What happened to Laura?" she said after she took another sip of coffee, not wanting the conversation to end.

"She hated the cold," Jim said. "She moved to Florida."

SAFE AS HOUSES

When he was a kid his mother told Jim Bates that houses had personalities. It wasn't necessarily the kind of thing that he would have thought of by himself, but once it had been said it couldn't be unsaid, or unthought, like realizing someone had nose hair or a slight limp and then seeing it every time you looked at them.

The house they had lived in was a friendly kind of house, a little too close to the road, with a porch running its whole width and a narrow dark blue door at its center. It was short and squat, and somehow that made it nice. It was like a lot of other houses on their road, and for a long time Jim thought of it as basically what all houses were like. Then one day they brought his father lunch at a house where he was doing the roof, and Jim realized that that wasn't so. That house was a haughty house, with a stained-glass eyebrow window above the double doors. Maybe it felt haughty to him because he could tell it was old, Victorian, the big rambling high-waisted house of people who could afford someone else to sweep the stairs and vacuum the parlor. Or maybe it was because his mother had packed a picnic lunch and his parents had perched on the back hatch of the station wagon with their ham sandwiches while he and Polly sat on the ground. A woman had come out wearing white gloves with pink flowers on them—gardening gloves, his mother said, which he thought was just about the stupidest thing he'd ever heard—carrying a set of big savage shears. "I didn't realize this was a family affair," she'd said with a smile that wasn't one, and his mother had flushed.

"Ice princess," his mother had muttered as she pulled away once lunch was done, looking in the rearview mirror.

"I liked her dress," Polly had whispered. She was four then.

From that day on Jim had really believed that people lived in houses that looked like them. Tad looked like one of the square Cape Cod houses in a patch of lawn on Upper Main, at least when he was in civilian clothes, and it so happened that that was where he lived and always had. Sarah should live in one of those tight little Dutch colonials with the sloping roofs, the ones that looked like their windows were winking at you, but she lived in a nondescript rented A-frame down a pitted gravel drive outside of town. Jim figured she lived in the A-frame because it looked like her husband, who was cheap and poorly made and beneath notice in exactly the way that house was.

"Forty-five dollars," he'd said, standing in front of Kevin at the gas station, and he could tell by the skittish way Kevin's eyes moved around that he knew exactly why Jim Bates was standing there with his big scarred palm out right under his nose. Kevin didn't have the money on him, which later, with a couple of beers in him, he'd convinced himself meant he would never have handed it over.

"You ever sell that woman, or anyone else, cheap fir as good firewood again, and you'll have to pull a log out of your ass to sit down," Jim Bates told him. Jim Bates never talked like that. He was famous for having a clean mouth in a dirty-mouth business.

"Screw you," Kevin said after the truck had already driven away.

Jim had seen houses that were a match for Rebecca only in photographs, the kind of upright, well-proportioned city house of brick or limestone that faced the street, faced right onto it but didn't give much away. Maybe she lived in a house like that in New York City. The house that she lived in here had no personality because it had never really had time to develop one. A local man had built it as a hunting cabin just after he got mustered out at the end of the Korean War, then decided what he really wanted to do was move south. He'd sold it to a couple who planned to start a camp in the area, but the strain of starting the business split them apart, and he went farther upstate (and started a lamp store) while she stayed for a year and then put the place back on the market.

It wasn't exactly insulated and it wasn't at all pretty, so it sat on the market for three years, more or less, and then a pair of young schoolteachers bought it because it was all they could afford. They toughed it out for ten years, but three bad winters in a row drove them into one of those small boxy houses in town, the kind of house that holds the heat in a tight fist. They rented the other place to some colleagues who stayed there two years and then bought forty acres farther out and built a big ranch house with a horse barn, although taking care of horses was a lot more work than they'd figured.

Then a book editor from New York had rented the house for the summer, and then for a year, then two, and finally bought it to use on weekends. When he'd died he left it to his lover, an architect. People said the architect sat on a stump in the woods all day long and sobbed. (It happened that this was true. He had loved the editor well and truly, although he frequently had sex with others.) So he decided to rent it out, and had, to a series of artists. Rebecca was the most recent short-term tenant.

It was like a foster house, passed from person to person without any love, maintenance, or decoration, a brown wood box with rattling windows and a toilet whose handle needed to be held down to flush. If Jim Bates owned it, he thought each time he pulled up at the door, he'd put a long porch on the front and a screened one on the back, put in bigger windows and add a kind of sunroom that would get light through the trees. Then he'd hang a bird feeder outside the sunroom, although he knew the bears would be inclined to tear it down.

As it was, it wasn't the right house for Rebecca Winter. It was too insubstantial, too unmarked. Jim liked objects that were what they seemed—a cookie jar that said COOKIES, not one designed to look like a bulldog, or a fat French chef. He thought Rebecca Winter looked like what she was. Maybe it was the dark clothes with no ruffles or fancy buttons, the shortish nails with no polish. Maybe it was her hair. He liked that it was plain, that she didn't do anything to it except stick it behind her ears when she was busy. As far as he could tell she didn't wear any makeup, although every once in a while she put stuff from a little round tin with roses on it on her lips, and when she did Jim always looked away, as though he was seeing something private.

"You always think that," Laura used to tell him, in the laughing voice that sounded a little too much like it was laughing at him. "You think women aren't wearing any makeup when the truth is that we just wear makeup in a way that looks like we're not wearing any makeup at all. That's the point."

If that was the point Laura had missed it. She wore stuff that turned her lashes navy blue and her eyelids lavender and her cheeks pink and her mouth pinker. Still, when he first met her he'd honestly believed she was a natural blonde.

If his theory about houses was correct, he should have known

it wasn't going to work out, even though she brought him pan-
cakes in bed and then did things with syrup she'd read about in
a magazine, even though she took Polly to the nail parlor for her
first pedicure and bought her a flowered bikini from a surf shop.
Laura wanted one of those new houses that looked like nobody
had ever lived there because nobody had, a two-story foyer with
a big showy brass light fixture on a chain, and a kitchen that was
part of a dining area that was part of a family room. She took
him to tour a model once, and he kept thinking of a sci-fi film
he'd seen when he was a kid, a guy in a room where the walls and
the ceiling were closing in on him in a way that was meant to be
scary. Jim actually wanted a house where the walls and ceiling
closed in a little bit more, like the house where he grew up, with
a kind of black scratchy mark in one corner of the living room
that showed the spot where the top of the Christmas tree always
grazed the ceiling and left a tattoo of evergreen gum.

When they'd wound up in that house after his father died,
Laura's beloved velvet sectional in the small square living room
had looked like a fat man in a shrunken suit. She'd tried, she
said, she'd really tried. But she wasn't cut out for

- small-town life,
- six months of winter,
- a teenage girl in the house.

Having his sister around had put a bit of a damper on the
stuff with the syrup, which had accounted for a fair amount of
the basis of their marriage, Jim discovered. Sometimes that was
the trouble, that Polly was there. And sometimes it was that
Polly was nowhere to be found and Jim had to go roust her from
some bar where she was using an ID she'd bought for twenty
bucks and dancing in a corner in a sports bra, whipping her shirt
around over her head. And that was on a good night.

Sometimes now it was like his marriage to Laura had never

even happened at all, and he thanked God for the invention of the birth control pill, which meant neither of them had wound up enmeshed in the kind of petty warfare over the hearts and minds of little kids Jim saw all around him: Mom says we can't have candy, Dad bought us Oreos, Mom says you didn't send the check, Dad says your boyfriend is an idiot. He'd been waiting in line at Arby's one day and he'd heard a little boy with a voice like a cartoon kitten say to the girl in cutoffs holding the hand of the man across the table from him, her chin in her hand, her foot tapping the vinyl tile floor, "My mommy says you're a hoochie."

He was sorry he'd never had kids. He was more than sorry; he was pretty brokenhearted about it, when he thought about it hard, which he tried not to do. But he was glad he hadn't had kids like that. It had been surprisingly easy; Laura had gone to see her mother in Nags Head and never come back. He'd packed up her stuff. "You can keep the sectional," she'd said. He hadn't, although it had been a bitch getting it out of the house, and he finally used a chain saw, which somehow made him feel better about things.

He got a Christmas card every year, first week in December like clockwork. Long blond hair (long fake-blond hair), serious tan, four authentically blond kids, balding husband with a gut in a golf shirt, big house, all in Orlando. The whole family, ranged along an aggressively ceremonial staircase in the two-story foyer with a tree in the curve of the stairs at the bottom. He wondered whether they put the tree up in October so they could take the picture, then put it away, then put it up again, like a dress rehearsal. No sap on the ceiling; the tree was silver, not even a second cousin of anything that grew in the forest. Laura looked like someone he'd never even met. He bet she'd say the same about him.

MERRY CHRISTMAS!

Oscar Winter and his neighbor, Levine from 6F—which is what he always called him, Levine from 6F—got a car service to take them three blocks to the movie theater to see the new James Bond. Then they went to the McDonald's for dinner. Levine had the Filet-O-Fish sandwich; Oscar had the Big Mac. "I never got the fuss about this special sauce," Oscar said, with special sauce on his chin. "It's French dressing, am I right?"

Sonya returned from dinner at her sister's house in Queens with a tin of homemade sugar cookies. "You're a saint!" Oscar said as he watched *How the Grinch Stole Christmas* and dunked the cookies into a glass of tea.

Ben went to a buffet supper at Amanda's parents' apartment. There were three trees: one with white lights in the living room, one with colored lights in the den, one covered with origami animals in the foyer. All had been done by a florist.

"I believe I know your father," Amanda's mother said a little stiffly, which made Ben wonder.

Sarah made bûche de noël for Kevin's family while Kevin, his brother, and his father watched sports on the TV in the paneled basement. After dinner they ate the entire bûche de noël, then went back downstairs, leaving the women to do the dishes. "You look like you've lost some weight, honey," Kevin's stepmother told Sarah.

Tad did a party in the children's wing of the cancer center in Nasserville. One little girl drew a picture of him with crayons and he put it on the refrigerator when he got home. "They should pay you!" his aunt said indignantly, taking his plate of baked ham and macaroni and cheese from the oven.

Jim Bates gave his sister, Polly, a white angora sweater. "It's a cloud," she said, holding it up. Then she put it on over her nightgown. "I'm tired," she said. "Yeah, I know, Pol," her brother said, putting the teakettle on.

Rebecca almost missed the day entirely. She lost track of time constantly these days, knew it was the weekend only because Jim Bates would fetch her in his truck, knew night was beginning to fall when the edges of the trees and the hem of the horizon blurred. She discovered it was Christmas because she went to Tea for Two first thing and found it closed. Closed, dark, silent, along with the hair salon, the insurance-travel-accounting agency, and all the other businesses downtown. The streets were deserted except for a young woman with a baby peeking quizzically from a front pack.

"The Gas-and-Go is open," the young woman said, holding up a cardboard cup of coffee. When she paused, the baby began to wail, so she started walking again, fast, slewing from side to side as though she was ice-skating on the sidewalk. All was calm as the young mother skated off toward the Methodist church.

The church bells began to play "O Holy Night." In her jeans pocket Rebecca's phone vibrated. There was a text from Ben: "Happy whatever we call it."

At the Jewish Home for the Aged and Infirm, Bebe Winter sat in the visitors' room and played all day. For whatever reason, she played the piano part of Handel's *Messiah*.

THIS IS HOW THESE THINGS
HAPPEN, PART ONE

Rebecca had printed out the cross pictures, which looked better and better to her each time she worked with them, and she had split a tuna melt with the dog, whom she was embarrassed to admit she called Dog when she called him at all. Giving him a name implied permanence and ownership, and she wasn't prepared to embrace either. Her building in New York forbids dogs over forty pounds, and while this dog looked half-starved when he arrived and is now still lanky, she can tell just by looking him over that he is heavier than that. He has eyes like black glass beads, and one ear that stands up like a cowlick after the other has fallen. He follows her everywhere, into the forest, around the house, but he doesn't like the idea of getting in the car. Twice that morning he had laid his head in her lap and looked up at her, and it was then that she thought about naming him, and realized that doing so made him one more brick in a wall that stood between her and her former existence.

"Don't become too attached," she said aloud, to one or the other of them.

It was too late; the dog had become attached. Perhaps it was the low even voice, the absence of screaming and hitting, the warm bedroom and the full food dish. Sometimes his ears would stiffen and Rebecca would imagine he was hearing something far away. This was correct; from the trailer at the bottom of the hill he could hear a quavering voice, its tremolo equal parts paranoia, distress, and medication, calling, "Jack! Jack, come back! Come home!" When Rebecca heard any of this at all she assumed it was the wind, which had picked up sharply since morning. The dog walked to the living room, turned in a circle, sank to the floor. A cold finger ran up his feathered spine, a sudden gust under the warped front door.

It had started snowing at midday, downy snow that picked up volume until the tree line was obscured by pale gray-white. Rebecca went out into it for about an hour, circling the woods and then walking down the drive to look in the mailbox. She had been looking for her latest check from the state, which was late or lost or merely tormenting her by keeping her waiting. The dog lifted his head to sniff the open mailbox. "Nothing," Rebecca said aloud.

When they turned back, flakes heavy on her lashes and the dog's muzzle, she saw that their tracks were being filled in swiftly. She had little experience of snow like this, that seized and overwhelmed its surroundings, wiping out all the sharp edges and landmarks. Snow in the city was a passing thing even when it was substantial, Central Park's peaks and gullies muted by a silvery glow at 5:00 A.M. and then slowly reappearing as the runners thumped the snow off the roads, the dog walkers tamped it down on the paths. In the city snow was as transient as a tourist. Here it stuck. Twice she heard a skittering noise that took her back to that night with the raccoon in the trap, then realized it was snow barreling down the slope of the roof.

It was a good day to stay inside, get some work done, throw the frozen turkey carcass from Thanksgiving in a big dented pot, the only really sizable pot in the house. The architect and the book editor had bought it one summer and brought it up from the city for a lobster feast that had gone awry because of too much Chardonnay, sun, and a certain sexual overlap between and among their friends of which they'd been unaware. Rebecca let the pot simmer bones into stock all day long, perfuming the house with something comforting and substantial. She defrosted some of the ground venison, too. Jim Bates had brought her a dozen packages of frozen meat and a bag of bones for the dog. "He seems like a good dog," he had said, looking him over while the dog sat at attention next to his truck, wagging his tail hard.

"He seems to like you," Rebecca had said, which was true.

She had been a little dispirited by the size of the venison portions; they were so conspicuously designed for a person alone, two small chops in some, a half pound of ground meat in others. And then she realized that that was how it had been packaged for Jim, that he would sit in the evening in that yellow kitchen and she at the dining room table here, each eating the solitary meal of a single person. She wondered if she should invite him to dinner, then dismissed it as too much. Lunch someday, perhaps.

She went to sleep early, slept long and heavily. When she finally woke, the dog was whimpering in the bedroom doorway, and the room had turned dull pewter. It was just after eight in the morning by her watch, and she jumped out of bed, the wood floor frosty on her feet. The dog was used to going out by six.

She pushed at the front door, but nothing happened. Again and again she tried, while the dog whimpered and then finally barked sharply. He'd peed on the floor in other houses, not wanting to but having no choice, and what happened after was painful and memorable. This woman seemed disinclined to hit him, but you never knew.

When Rebecca gave up and looked out the window, she saw a moonscape around her, the path, the steps, even the car wiped out by enormous drifts of snow. Several breached the bottoms of the windows, and a light powdering inside showed where the sills fit ill.

In the back bedroom she found a window that opened. When she shoved it up the snow blew in, and the dog heaved up and hopped out. He was instantly buried to his shoulders, and Rebecca stood and watched as he weaved around the deeper drifts over to the tree line and into the forest, where the canopy was weighed down low and white and the ground was a bit clearer. He tried to lift a leg, put it down, satisfied himself with squatting, went a little farther until he was just a sandy back and neck, then returned. It was still snowing hard, and what was already on the ground was blowing fitfully in a steady series of strong gusts.

For the first few hours it felt like an adventure, the two of them alone in the deep deep silence, not of the house but of its surroundings, muffled completely by the snow batting in which they found themselves wrapped. Rebecca was pretty certain of the location of her car, but if it was where she thought it was it had been completely buried by a drift that butted up against the shed. Twice more she opened the back window for the dog, but by the second time the snow was even higher and tipped off the sill and into the room, melting on the splintery floor. Sleep that night was not so deep, and toward dawn, or what she thought was dawn—like the aurora borealis, the glowing snow had turned the edges of night into a strange imitation of day—she felt the dog tentatively climb onto the end of the bed, and she didn't push him off. The house smelled like turkey stock and woodsmoke, and she ran over in her mind how much food in cans she had in the cabinets, and as she did that she realized that she was completely alone, cut off from everything around her, and that that was a feeling she had had living within her for a long long time without allowing herself to recognize it.

In the morning she pushed the snow off the outside sill of the window with a dustpan, and hoisted the dog over the edge. He fell into a drift, and pushed his muzzle deep into it. He could manage only a few steps, doing his business with his head down as though he was ashamed to have so little privacy. She couldn't know that it reminded him of all the times he'd looked for a fresh spot to squat when his range was circumscribed by a length of chain and a choke collar. He managed to put his paws on the outside sill, and she hoisted him in by his front legs and gave him half of an English muffin. Since she so often ate at Tea for Two, the poor store-bought muffin was a little hard at one edge.

She put the light on under the stock again just for the heat and the smell, put another log on the fire, and realized as she did that the six others stacked nearby were all she had. There was a whole wall of wood against one side of the house, split and stacked, but all of it was under snow like her car and the snow shovel leaning useless against one wall of the shed. She was overwhelmed by her own stupidity and helplessness. She had a phone and a computer, neither of which worked in this house. Somewhere a few miles down the mountain there were scones, and espresso, and cell service, but they might as well be in Tibet. Or, she supposed, on West Seventy-Sixth Street, which seemed just as far away.

"It has to melt at some point," she said to the dog, who lifted that one rebellious ear, then laid himself down flat as a throw rug.

She worked for a few distracted hours, reprinting more of the cross pictures, looking at the images taken from different angles. For an hour after lunch she took pictures of the dog, the hard scarred pads of his paws, the rough fur of his back, finally his face, full-on. He seemed to understand his function; he cocked

his head, turned it slightly, raised a brow like a cartoon character. With no one to hear her but him, Rebecca said, "This is what
it's come to. Birds and dogs. Next I will be shooting weddings. I
will be working for a studio that takes the high school graduation photos." The dog listened carefully. He liked it better when
she was not unhappy.

Just before four o'clock, with two fast flickers and the asth-
matic wheeze of the old refrigerator, the power went off, and
in the half-light she closed her eyes and sighed. "Candles," she
said. But there were none. Of course.

THIS IS HOW THESE THINGS
HAPPEN, PART TWO

For the rest of her life Rebecca Winter would apprehend the rumble of a truck engine in deep silence, or anything dimly like it, even the rhythmic solo roll of a kettledrum in a symphonic passage, as the soothing sound of salvation.

It was past nightfall by the time she heard it, but how far she could not have said. For hours she sat in the dark, with nothing to do except think of things, so that her thoughts covered a world tour of subjects: whether the cross photographs were enigmatic or merely confusing, whether her work would still sell again at slightly or greatly reduced prices, whether she could sell the New York apartment for enough money to live on for the foreseeable future, whether Ben would be bereft if she sold it, whether she could bear to live outside Manhattan, whether she should live closer to her father, what the Mary Cassatt was worth, what her own life was worth now that it felt oddly like someone else's life. She thought for the first time in years of being pregnant, and how her body had once felt as though it no longer belonged to her and yet was more hers than it had ever been before (or after). "I'm gobsmacked by those men who say they are aroused by a pregnant woman," Peter had said, in that way in which he insisted he was merely being factual when he was really being cruel.

She was thinking of Peter, wondering whether the sex and his accent were enough to explain why she had married him (they were, if you threw in the way he read poetry, which was related to both), when she heard the truck climbing the driveway. The spotlights of headlights ran across the front windows, asking a semaphore question, and the dog barked an answer. Rebecca ran to throw open the door before remembering that this was impossible. On tiptoes she could see the very top of the blade of a plow illuminated, yellow as a taxicab, by the lights of the truck. For an hour it moved back and forth, back and forth, like a student driver learning to perform a K-turn, until there were mountains of snow interrupted by flat areas of drive and battered grass. Then there was the scraping of a shovel against the door, and with her on one side and Jim Bates on the other, pushing, pulling, pushing, pulling, the door finally came open, and the harsh winter wind blew in and scattered dead ashes across the stone hearth.

"Damn," he said, ice on his eyebrows and lashes. "I thought you were asleep. The place is pitch black." He stomped snow off his boots on the threshold. "Ah, hell," he said. "No power?"

"None whatsoever," Rebecca said, twisting her odd mouth in a way that made his heart stutter-stop. What she thought looked wry he read as scared and sad. He was right.

"Wait," he said and waded back into the cold, and the black, and the silver-white night, turned off the truck, and pulled something from behind the driver's seat.

"One Coleman lantern," he said as he put it on the dining table, where it cast a small but somehow unearthly glow, like the last fire in the last place on earth.

The dining room table in the home of a person living alone becomes the entire world, divided into countries: the area for the mail, for work if there is any, a small duchy set aside for the placement of one dish, one bowl, one fork. Rebecca looked at her table in the wan yellow light of the lantern and saw her life in all of its loneliness, and when he looked up she could see it reflected in his face. It was the first time he had been inside her house since he had rousted the raccoon, and it felt entirely different than it had that day, when she was a customer and he a hired man.

"Thank you," she muttered, as though she was dismissing him.

"You haven't yet begun to thank me," he said and pulled a bottle from inside his parka. "Tullamore Dew," it said.

"Behold," he said, as his eyebrows thawed and made rivulets down his pink face.

She couldn't remember the last time she had had whiskey, or even alcohol. In the beginning she had had wine with her dinner, but the solitary glass, the recorked bottle—both had underlined what she thought of as her exile. The Tullamore Dew had a pretty name, was a pretty color, was smooth and easy, particularly after the first jelly glass full. She put her head back against the tired lumpy couch and listened to him talk, about how there was so much snow that Sarah had had to keep Tea for Two closed, about the ninety-seven-year-old woman on Creek Road he'd plowed out, who'd given him half a pie and two dollars—"one in quarters, if you can believe it"—about how the snow had brought down the roof of the volunteer fire station and he'd be working on that as soon as the weather cleared, although he didn't like to do flat roofs.

He didn't tell her how Tad had called him and said, "Do you

think Ms. Winter is safe up there on her own?" and he'd said, "Ah, hell," because he'd gotten so busy plowing out his sister's place and the woman on Creek Road and the Methodist church where they had the AA meetings that he'd left it too long, maybe because he thought Rebecca was as self-sufficient a person as he'd ever known, despite not knowing when there was a raccoon in the attic and buying firewood from that idiot Kevin.

"You still awake?" he said finally, when he got exhausted filling the silence, a little worried that he'd been rambling in that way people who know they've had a lot to drink do. He hadn't had a lot to eat, he realized, as he smelled turkey, and the whiskey was running a little wild inside him because of that. It was getting cold, too. No power, no furnace. He poked the logs in the fireplace.

"Not entirely," said Rebecca finally, her eyes faint glimmers at the bottom edges of her lids, and something about that, the spark in the dark, made him lean down and kiss her, a Tullamore Dew kiss that, in the way of semidrunken kisses, got very wet very fast. He was really enjoying himself until suddenly, as though all the languor and relief of being rescued had disappeared in an instant, Rebecca pulled back—no, when she thought of it afterward, ever afterward, she realized she had recoiled, and she was mortified and remorseful.

But that was later.

He pressed himself back against her and she pressed back with her hands, hard.

"What?" he said.

"What?"

"What?"

"Never mind," she said, standing up and sidestepping a bit as she did, with a small stumble that was either the Dew or nerves or both. "This is ridiculous. How old are you?"

"What difference does that make? You're making this way more complicated than it needs to be. It doesn't need to be complicated." She looked fierce, the way handsome women do when they are confused, or angry, or embarrassed, or all three.

"I was forty-four last month," he finally said, putting his glass down emphatically.

"Oh my God."

"Yeah, you missed my birthday."

"That's not the point. Forty-four? Oh my God."

"Would fifty have been better?"

"I'm sixty years old."

"Right. So what? You look great. Is that what I'm supposed to say?"

"What?"

"In my experience, if women tell you how old they are it's so you'll tell them how good they look."

"That was not why I told you how old I was. It was so you would understand how ridiculous it would be to—"

"What?"

"What?"

"Ridiculous?"

"Ludicrous."

"Ludicrous. Hell, that's even worse than ridiculous," he said, and with what seemed to be one motion he grabbed his dripping parka and walked back out into the snow. In what seemed to be one mental motion, Rebecca hoped that his truck would start, and that it wouldn't.

It did. The rumble of salvation became fainter and fainter. The dog whined and circled the room. Rebecca sat back down on the couch, heavily. For most of her life she had not been what anyone would call an emotional person, but at odd, quiet, unexpected times—the climax of an old film, a passage in a book, even the occasional insurance ad—sentiment got the better of her.

"Oh, my goodness," she said and burst into tears, and sobbed loudly.

For a moment or two she consoled herself with the notion that she was drunk, but it was as little consolation as it had been to most sensitive people over time, although the hard-hearted used it for everything from meanness to manslaughter. The dog licked her face and made a sympathetic noise in his throat that sounded like a rusty hinge. The wind blew down the chimney. Rebecca cried, and cried some more. The Coleman lantern flickered slightly, turning the glass of whiskey Jim Bates had left next to it into a prism.

Then the dog stepped back, sat down at attention, and let out one sharp bark. In a moment she heard the sound he'd heard, with his sharper ears, and wiped hard at her face with the side of her hand as she stood up. When the door opened so much snow blew in that there was a small storm in the living room.

"This is ludicrous," Jim said, and without removing his parka he put his arms around her and kissed her and kissed her, wet and cold and covered with snow as he was, until he had backed her into the dark bedroom and closed the door shut in the dog's face.

WHAT CAME NEXT—HER

When she woke it was 7:00 A.M. The dog had been fed, the coffee made. Rebecca had not ever used, nor much heard used in conversation, the expression "feels like a million bucks." But for some reason it was circling around her head like the digital news ribbon in Times Square:

Rebecca Winter Feels Like a Million Bucks. Rebecca Winter Feels Like a Million Bucks.

The bottle of Tullamore Dew sat on the dining room table with half an inch still in the bottom. She smiled at the bottle, felt foolish, got coffee, sat on the couch, and thought of various episodes from the previous night. The power had come back on just before daybreak, so that suddenly the two of them were pinned down by an unforgiving overhead light with a hundred-watt bulb, and not the soft-light kind, either. The dark, the dark, the utter dark had been her friend as she considered the slackness at the tops of her haunches, the cesarean scar on her belly, the creased skin of her cleavage. She had always been small-breasted, and all her life she had hated it until, in locker rooms looking around at the other middle-aged swimmers struggling out of their maillots, she had realized that gravity was more charitable to the flat-chested.

Jim had gotten up to turn off the light, and when he returned he said happily, "Wow," which was exactly the right thing to say. Fifteen minutes later they were both asleep again.

"Don't get up," he said an hour later when he pulled on his pants in the half-light.

She looked out the window. The truck was gone, the snow had mostly stopped falling. Her head hurt, but not as much as she would have expected. She put on her boots and went out with the dog. With the path cleared, the drive plowed, the snow that had seemed so terrifying and overwhelming the day before now seemed merely beautiful. The sky, the ground, the roof and trees, everything was one color, one faintly translucent and glowing shade of white, and it was beautiful in a way that no photograph could ever capture. A few flakes continued to fall, dipping, wheeling, what she'd learned in the tree stand to call riding the zephyrs.

Rebecca made a snowball and tossed it into the air, and the dog tried to catch it and looked befuddled when it turned to dust in his jaws, and so she did it again and again, laughing, thinking about Jim Bates and how happy he'd looked when he got up to turn out the light. She was a sixty-year-old woman: she knew that she was supposed to be remembering what went here and there, who did what to whom, except that the truth is, what goes here and there and who does what to whom changes very little from event to event, even under the best of circumstances.

And while she was indeed thinking of some of that, she mainly remembered how Jim Bates had looked in that unpleasant overhead glare for just a minute, the look a small boy has on his face at the head of the table when his mother walks in with the birthday cake, candles lit. She liked the feeling that she was the cake. She'd had sex before, many times, good and bad and indifferent, too. But she'd never before felt like the cake.

He'd left a note on the table: "back tonight with lasagna." She wondered what she would do when he walked in with the casserole dish. She wondered when and whether they would eat. All day long she rehearsed what she would say: Hello. Come in. Come right in. Oh my goodness. Oh my dear God. (She had said that at some point during the night, maybe more than once.) Go away. Please go away. Please stay. Everything sounded equally stupid. Maybe she should just open the door and see what happened next.

What happened next was nothing. There was no lasagna, no casserole dish, no Jim Bates. "Wow," and then he was gone.

WHAT HAPPENED NEXT—HIM

He went to his sister Polly's house. It was a little jumped-up trailer on a piece of land with bad drainage and stony soil that someone had given Jim's grandfather in trade for a new roof, years and years before Jim was born, and it had sat flat and empty and derelict until Jim bought a trailer and had it towed there. He had tried to make it pretty, with shutters and fresh paint and trelliswork around the foundation so you couldn't see the concrete blocks. He'd plowed its stubby driveway the night before, before he'd plowed Rebecca's driveway and then had the time of his life. But he hadn't gone inside because all the lights were out, which meant his sister was blessedly asleep. Sometimes she stayed up for three or four days on end, and his phone would ring at all hours, ten, twelve times a night: Jimmy, do you remember? Jimmy, can you come? Jimmy, I hate you. Jimmy, I love you. When he'd seen the dull sheen of white paint against the white snow with no yellow glare from inside, no moving silhouette across the windows—pace, pace, stop, stare out, stare down, pace, pace—he'd felt relieved. He'd felt like he was free, for one night at least. That's how he'd felt when he drove up the hill to the cottage. That's how he'd behaved, like a free man.

There was no sign of life in the dim morning light. No smoke from the pipestem chimney, no glow from the light in the cheap hood over the narrow stove. His sister had had a dog, the dog that Rebecca had now, but Jim liked dogs and he knew his sister was an unreliable owner so he hadn't said a thing to either of them. Sometimes Polly remembered the dog, sometimes not. Sometimes she'd completely forgotten about him. Often she'd completely forgotten to feed him. The dog had filled out since he'd moved on to Rebecca's place.

Jim went inside. His head hurt, but not as much as he would have expected. He whistled through his teeth, and the whistle came out as a plume of white smoke. It was cold in the house. The sink was filled with dishes. His sister liked pie. Ice cream, too. It was hard to get her to eat decent food. It was like whatever lived inside her craved sugar, like a tapeworm. He wished it had been a tapeworm. Then the doctors could have gotten it out.

The bed hadn't been slept in. That good feeling he'd had from head to toe since he climbed out of the lumpy bed up the hill, like he had hot fingerprints from his feet to his face, went away in an instant, and now he was cold all over. He saw an odd shadow on the window, went closer, and saw there was a ladder against the back of the house. For some reason the snow had drifted off to one side of it, so the area around the ladder was pretty clear. It was the kind of thing his sister always took as a sign of some kind or another.

Jim could go up a ladder fast but never as fast as he did that morning.

If you didn't know the flat roof of the trailer it looked pretty much like the flat roof of a trailer after a bad snowstorm. But if you looked closely you could see what looked like a snow angel near the middle, only instead of concave, it was convex. He dug with his hands. Her skin was pinker than the snow, but not much.

For the second time that day he took a woman he loved irrationally into his arms and held her tight to warm her up. The second time it didn't take.

POLLY BATES

Ah, Polly Bates. What a pretty little girl she'd been, the sort of blond, round-faced little girl who becomes accustomed to people remarking on how adorable she is, which often makes what comes after so painful, the metamorphosis from wheat yellow hair to mouse brown, from chubby cheeks to fat face. She was ten when her mother died, although all of that dying stuff was only words, as far as she was concerned: no one took her to the hospital or the funeral home or the cemetery. It was all considered too upsetting for a child. Her brother argued otherwise, but conventional wisdom prevailed, which was how she wound up thinking that her mother had merely packed up and moved away, perhaps impressed by a TV news story at the time about a woman who had done just that, left her five sons behind with their father and turned up later in Portland, selling real estate.

When she was twelve Jim joined the Marines and was gone, more or less, until she was sixteen and their dad died. Emergency room, funeral home, graveside: this time she knew dead was dead. It took Jim about a month, back home with his new bride, to realize why everyone shut up when he walked into a bar or a bait shop. He put it down at first to their dad dying, the fact that they were orphans now, although the word sounded a little dramatic as far as he was concerned. It was his wife who figured out that Polly had been having sex with everyone from the guy who sat next to her in homeroom to the mechanic who fixed her car to the softball coach, who had triplets and no hair to speak of. She wasn't picky, Polly. "The town bicycle," Laura had said, "everybody's had a ride," and Jim came as close to hitting her as he ever had come to hitting a woman, before or since, even including Polly at her worst. By the time her dad died Polly had lost count of how many guys there had been, and some she couldn't even remember, in part because she was usually pretty hammered when it was happening. There were drugs, too. Jim decided to send her to a place, a nice place near the Canadian border that looked more like a B-and-B than a rehab. It wiped out his savings and he took a second mortgage on the house.

And that's when Polly got sober, swore off sex, and began to talk about the voices in her head, and on the car radio, and from the squirrels in the woods, and the little china figurines on the shelf in the living room. When she stopped drinking and smoking pot it finally became clear: she was, in the words of those silent bar goers trying not to look her big brother in the eye, totally batshit. Not always, and not when she was taking the meds, which made her fat and lazy and stupid, so that when crazy daylight peeked around the edges of the pills she would stash them in the pockets of her housecoat and welcome her delusions back home. That's when she would write, pages and pages of stuff that made no sense at all, about murders and rapes and the existence of God and the end of the world.

"You ever do crazy Polly?" someone would say at the bar, but only after they'd looked around to make sure Jim wasn't there.

There's a kind of casual cruelty in a small town, but there's casual kindness, too. There wasn't a lot of talk about Polly after the first few years; the situation settled into silence in deference to her brother. Sarah had gotten wind of Polly when she first came to town, and in her Sarah way she had asked a lot of questions until one morning the woman who ran the beauty salon said quietly, "I think you might want to leave that alone, sweetie." And so she did.

Even when people couldn't leave it alone most of them tried to be nice about it. Jim would get home from work and listen to the messages on the phone, and sometimes there would be one about Polly: Jim, hon, it's Elaine Wallenchinsky over at the tow shop? I'm not sure, but I think I just saw your sister on the road in her nightie. Although maybe it's just a sundress, I was going pretty fast, rear-ender on the highway, you know, so I was trying to make up some time. Maybe take a look? Anyhow. That new downspout is a godsend.

There'd been two golden years in there, years when a doctor had tried a new potpourri of pills and the thunderstorm between his sister's ears seemed to die down to occasional rain. She worked as an aide at the senior center, began to go out with someone who had been a few years ahead of her in high school, a mechanic named Craig who put up with the snickers in exchange for regular meals, companionship, and the occasional sexual experience, since the meds that cleared Polly's mind shut down her sex drive. They moved into the white trailer outside of town, at the bottom of the steep slope, and Polly planted impatiens and potato vines in two old cedar planters she found at the Salvation Army store and got an orange-and-white cat. Then something happened. The plants died from lack of water, the cat ran off, and Craig moved out after she kept waking him in the middle of the night to ask did he hear, did he hear the whispers, did he hear the people in the other room, the murderers, the rap-ists? "I got to get some sleep," he told Jim. "She can keep the TV if she wants."

"Come home," Jim said, but she sat on the couch, nodding off from the new meds, shaking her head slowly from side to side with her eyes at half-mast.

Three times he almost lost her. Once she stabbed herself in the thigh. Once she went under in the tub. Once she took too many pills. Accidents, she told him after in the hospital.

Every evening his sister got into bed with the pink stuffed bear Jim had won her at the Blueberry Festival the month before he'd gone into the service. She'd taken the bear up onto the roof with her. If she woke up she would say that was an accident, too, that she'd gone up there to look at the stars, to look at the storm, or, if it had been a bad night, to get away from the people who were breaking into the house, finally coming down the hill to get her. But she didn't wake up.

THE STORM

The way Rebecca had lived during the storm was the way she lived after it. The way she had lived for the two days before Jim Bates showed up to plow was the way she lived for weeks on end, like someone under house arrest, wearing one of those ankle bracelets. She stayed in the cottage, she tried to work, she read some old books—*Moby-Dick, Swann's Way,* the kinds of books you always meant to read and somehow never had. It was hard to get out, with the snow and the ice and the steep and curving country roads, and she avoided town most of the time, going to Tea for Two only occasionally now. She was afraid that if she ran into Jim Bates she would hiss "Lasagna?" For some reason it was the lasagna that especially rankled her, with its implied promise of domesticity and caring. It was one thing to have a man sleep with you and then disappear;

it was quite another when he'd explicitly said he'd be back and bring dinner.

She photographed the dog over and over again, until when she would go into the back room to get her cameras he would sit expectantly in front of the couch, waiting. Lie down, she said. Stand up. Look here. He was a very intelligent dog. He knew exactly what she needed. Every night he heaved himself to the foot of the bed, to one side of Rebecca's legs, so that he gave off a little warmth, as though she wasn't really alone at all. Even though she felt as alone as she'd ever felt before. Sometimes it was like that whole night was something she'd read about, or imagined, except that in the back of the cupboard above the refrigerator there was a bottle of Tullamore Dew with a glimmer of gold in its wide bottom. She kept thinking she should heave it in the trash.

It's a funny thing, hope. It's not like love, or fear, or hate. It's a feeling you don't really know you had until it's gone.

Three more nights there were big storms, although not as big as that first one, and she heard the sound of someone plowing her drive. She sat, and shivered, and breathed deeply in a way that made the dog sit in front of her and stare into her face. But she didn't turn on any more lights, and she sure as hell didn't go to the door of the cabin. She'd learned her lesson. Ludicrous. Ha!

Nearly every day she forced herself to walk in the woods, the dog following a trail of scent ahead of her. She always brought her cameras, but it often happened that when they'd returned she couldn't really remember where they'd gone or what they'd seen, and she hadn't taken any photographs at all. There had been no more crosses, or at least none that she had found, even when the snow on the ground had mostly melted away. Twice, by mistake, or at least she believed it was by mistake, she found herself near the tree stand, but she could tell by the mounded snow atop the plywood platform that no one had been there in a long time.

One afternoon she was working with the cross pictures and deciding which to send to TG when she heard a truck climbing the driveway, struggling against the slope. The dog let out a sharp gruff bark, and she moved from the table to sit on the couch, one hand knotted in the other. The truck stopped; she heard its door open, then close. When there was a knock at the door it was as though every thought she could possibly have scrambled through her mind in just an instant, like a squirrel through the leaves in the woods.

"It's been a long time since I've delivered here," said the UPS man. "Boy, it's a slog."

That was a bad day. That, and the day Tad drove up with the back of his car filled with a bouquet of pink balloons. The balloons crowded into the living room, bumping against the ceiling, mobbing the fireplace. When she looked at the card, it said, "Happy Valentine's Day from Tad."

"Would you like a cup of tea?" she asked, and with a bow Tad said, "That would be very nice."

As they sat at the table she realized, by the way the bunch of balloons bounced from one end of the room to another, that she must have a leaky window or a break in the walls. The day before she had found a shingle on the ground. "I need a roofer," she told the dog, with a harsh laugh that made his ears come down. She sent the owner of the cottage an email, but he did not respond.

("What does she think, that for a thousand a month she's getting the Taj Mahal?" he said to one of his friends on a sunny terrace in Bermuda, where he was overseeing an addition to a hotel.)

"I hope you won't take it amiss if I say that you have been an inspiration to me," Tad said. "Those"—he nodded at the balloons, which seemed to nod back—"are a small token."

"That's lovely, but unnecessary," she replied.

"By example. You've inspired me by example. I have considered for a long time changing my life. Drastically, as it happens. Your example has told me that that is possible."

"I haven't made much of a change," she said, bending her face to her teacup as the ribbons from the balloon bouquet passed overhead, touched her cheek, and moved away.

"Adaptation," Tad said. "I required a model of adapting to new circumstances. I thank you for providing that."

"Can you share your plans?" she asked, thinking, Oh, no, please don't, don't make me listen to one of those scenarios so clearly doomed to failure, the lovely home cook who decides to launch a line of cookies, the venture capitalist who has always wanted to own a country inn.

"They are in flux, but you will be the first to know," Tad said, and again she thought, Oh no. Please don't. Please.

"This is excellent tea," he added.

"Lipton's," she said.

"My mother has always favored it."

She'd told Ben the story of the snowstorm, leaving out the last few hours, of course, and he'd said, "Ah, man, Mom, no cell, no email? You can't be that out of the communications loop." The UPS man had brought a package from Ben, a little plastic divot she put into one side of her computer. She didn't know how it worked, but it meant that, on a semiregular basis, she was able to get email at the house. This was less momentous than perhaps her son believed. She heard from Dorothea, who was on a yearlong teaching fellowship in Venice and who appeared to be having a good time, although Rebecca was skeptical of this because she knew the emails she sent in return had likely convinced Dorothea that she was having a good time, too.

There were photographs of houses she might use during the semester at Carnegie Mellon, small but pretty, with porches and pocket lawns. There was one that she thought she would choose, and each time she looked at it, and at the tentative schedule of lectures, seminars, graduate tutorials, she felt like an actor preparing for a role: for a term she would turn herself back into that strange familiar version of herself, the clothes in the closet in rotation again. She sent a message, took the house, confirmed the schedule. The artist formerly known as Rebecca Winter.

She checked her bank balance once a day, as though it might have magically changed overnight, and change it slowly did, but only for the worse. As for the rest: invitations, the occasional press inquiry, some requests for speeches at art schools and women's clubs. One lunch invitation for the birthday of a friend.

It was funny, what friendship meant in Rebecca's world. It mainly meant lunch, twice a year, and the occasional dinner party, except for Dorothea, who was an old school friend, a genuine friend. Rebecca had realized, ruefully, that she should have made more friends in school; they seemed to be the only ones women really talked to honestly because the shared history meant fewer lies were available to them. With the others shared meals had become a substitute for intimacy, but not the kind of substitute that allowed for dark nights of the soul, calls at 1:00 A.M., tears and drinking and despair in pajamas. How many times had she heard women in New York—maybe women everywhere, for all she knew—speak lyrically of how they wouldn't see friends for months, perhaps even years, and then it was as though they had never been apart. "Picked up where we left off" was the common phrase. It was supposed to signal some magical communion, but if you looked it right in the eye, it came down to this: the kinds of people they considered friends they might not even actually see for a long long time.

It seemed so far away, all of it, although she knew that if she got into the car and drove for two hours she would be in the city, in Central Park or at the museums. The idea gave her vertigo. She went for days without speaking, unless she talked to the dog. When the ground was clear of snow, or clear enough, the two of them might hike for hours. When she pulled on her jeans one morning she noticed that her legs were as hard as firewood, that the muscles of her thighs made vertical lines reaching to the bend of her pelvis. There was a sharp suggestion of rib above her waist. Some nights when she couldn't be bothered to cook venison she ate tuna right from the can, or a bowl of lukewarm black beans, while the dog stared up into her face, his tail a metronome. Please please please. She always shared.

One early morning the two of them struck out up the mountain until Rebecca realized that they were farther than she'd ever come before. Pushing through a stand of denuded brambles, their sharp nails reaching for her jacket, she came upon a long flat plain and saw railroad tracks disappearing into the distance. Sometimes at night she heard the lowing of a train whistle; this must be its source, the kind of ramshackle tracks that carried occasional freight through the outskirts of towns. She and the dog followed the tracks until what looked like the end of the world appeared at their juncture, and she saw that the earth fell away to a rocky chasm with a stream working its way across the bottom. The tracks continued over a trestle that threaded its way above nothing to the other side. Rebecca stopped at its edge to take a few photographs, and then she began to walk across it.

Lying in bed that night she would think about why. She was not afraid of heights but neither was she adventurous. She could ski intermediate slopes but didn't care to, knew how to snorkel but had never learned to scuba dive, had never feared flying but didn't care for small planes. When she had looked at the photographs after, it had seemed the thrust of the tracks disappearing into woods beyond the enormous opening in the land demanded exploration.

But the truth was that the sudden disappearance of the solid ground beneath her feet had felt like a laugh in her face, a declaration of war, a cosmic bet that she could not and would not and didn't dare, as though it made visible where she had wound up and how she felt about that. She was shaking slightly as she began, and it was with anger. And, almost halfway across the long trestle, she looked down, and the shaking was adrenaline. She fell to her knees on the wooden crossbars, through which she could see the stream and the rocks and the drop to both, and she could feel herself tumbling in her own imagination. She climbed the trestle like a ladder back to where she had begun, hand over hand, until she threw herself onto the frozen solid ground where she had started. The dog licked her face. He had not budged.

Oh, the loneliness, the loneliness. It lived inside her now like an illness, like a flu that could be ignored and then would suddenly overtake and overwhelm her. If she'd fallen from the railroad trestle she wondered how long it would have been before anyone had even known, who would have cared, who would have mourned. She could almost see the story in the *Times*, with a photograph of her photograph, alongside, or perhaps in lieu of, a photograph of her face. "Rebecca Winter," they would say in galleries and restaurants. "You didn't hear? An accident, I guess. Or maybe . . . well, things were difficult." Sometimes she felt as though she was disappearing, that she was being whittled down to just this terrible feeling, like a sudden aching that appeared all over, not in her body but in her soul. At night she woke: 1:23, 3:07, 4:22, blurry advertisements from the little digital clock. And when she could not go back to sleep: 1812 in the checking account, 740 for the car insurance, the 400 from the state that hadn't yet cleared her account. It was funny, how her equations had come to rely on 200 here, 200 there, the 200 she would no longer have since she would not be sitting in a tree with Jim Bates if hell froze over, which, some days, it seemed likely to do. She was never very good at math; now she was haunted by numbers, filling the black hours after the sun went down.

On her next birthday, sixty-one.

As she hiked back to the cabin, the dog nudging along her thigh as though concerned, she remembered a night years ago when she had been lying in bed in her apartment in New York, reading, and through the wall had heard the sound of someone weeping and wailing. They were thick walls, in the old building, which meant that the sound at its starting point must be loud for her to hear it. She had pressed her ear to the plaster as the sound died, stuttered back into life, began again. Something in her had wanted to call 911, to whisper into the phone, someone's heart is breaking in apartment 8C. What a silly thought. The police could never keep up with it, with all the breaking hearts behind the locked doors of New York City apartments. She imagined that the woman had lost her lover, or her job, or her best friend, or had just found herself broken by the weight of her own life. There were a thousand ways to imagine someone unhappy and so few ways to imagine someone contented.

The next day in the elevator she had seen the woman who lived in 8C. She was wearing a black suit with a big brooch on the shoulder, and carrying a lipstick-red bag that matched her shoes, and she gave Rebecca a toothy smile. Rebecca smiled back. So much smiling in the service of pretense. Alone in the cottage she needn't smile, and didn't.

Sometimes she realized that when she had been married, at the height of her success, her days had been filled with tasks: Ben to preschool, a meeting with a gallery owner, a dinner order at the fish store, a stop at the dry cleaner for the dress for the cocktail party. She had had time for thoughts only at night, as she lay in bed, Peter's back a clamshell in striped cotton beside her. She had had a hard time sleeping in those days because of all her thoughts. Was Ben's failure to achieve word recognition a sign of some learning disability? Did his biting phase mean he was unhappy? Was he unhappy because his father sniped at his mother? Did Peter snipe at her because they had not had decent sex for a month, or had they not had decent sex for a month because he sniped at her? What had he meant when he said he found her work derivative? Surely he'd only been in a mood.

Surely it meant he didn't love her. Surely it meant she was no good at her work.

No wonder she hadn't been able to sleep. There had been bees in her brain, a whole hive, no honey. Now her thoughts were a daytime thing, and there were fewer specific questions and more general ones. What would happen next? How and where would she live? How could she make a living? She knew any reasonable person would say she should downsize, down-grade, sell her apartment, but that was if you thought of an apartment as real estate instead of a home. She didn't want to sell her home. She thought of it as the last link to the self she had once been.

She felt foolish and yet somehow as though she had woken up to something that she should have known long ago. She remembered how Dorothea had told her, and only her, not to bring her a snow globe ever again. When Dorothea was in college some-one had given her one, and she was charmed by it, and had started a collection. Soon everyone who knew her knew, that for a birthday or a holiday or simply a dinner party offering, they could bring her a snow globe. Except that Dorothea was no lon-ger charmed by snow globes; they took up space, developed a milky patina of dust, and after a while all looked the same. But it was still the case that, with a certain sort of smile, someone would say to her, "I've found the perfect thing for your birth-day."

"Another goddamned snow globe," Dorothea would mutter.

People froze you in place, Rebecca sometimes thought, trudg-ing through the woods. More important, you froze yourself, often into a person in whom you truly had no interest. So you had a choice: you could continue a masquerade, or you could give up on it. No matter what Tad might think about her skill at adaptation, it was hard to know how to do that.

There were nights when she woke with a barbed-wire fence of minor but undeniable pain around her heart, and she rehearsed what she'd eaten that day—raisin bran, peanut butter and jelly sandwich, chicken and rice, the cuisine of a freshman at boarding school—and convinced herself that it was indigestion, then wondered if she was having the female version of a heart attack, which she had been told was often overlooked, which seemed right since her experience was that women overlooked most of what their hearts told them. In the morning she felt fine except for the fact that she had made her hands into little paws beneath her cheek and they had gone numb at the wrists. In recent years what she missed most about her youth was sleep, that ability to fall into a hole of unconsciousness and land, softly and without sensation, at the bottom, to awake ten hours later rested and with skin remarkably uncreased.

The night she'd tried to cross the railroad trestle she slept as deeply as she had for years. Just at dawn she woke to the sound of the train whistle, then went back to sleep and slept two hours more.

WHAT IN THE WORLD WAS THAT?

She finally bought a space heater. The furnace was a sad little thing, nearly fifty years old; when the plumber finally replaced it, the following year, he said, "That sucker wouldn't heat a dog-house." Even a good fire in the fireplace reached only to one end of the couch, leaving the small hallway and the kitchen frigid. The bedroom had newish windows, but even there Rebecca sometimes slept in a sweatshirt.

But it took her most of the winter to shake the feeling that a space heater represented an even more marked fall in the world than her thoughts about dipping into her retirement account. For some reason her parents had been obsessed, in a small way, with space heaters; she wondered now if both had childhood memories of visits to relatives with crowded walk-up apartments and a glowing death trap in one corner of the living room. She knew only that, from time to time, her mother would read the newspaper and say caustically to her father, as though he had lit the match, "Four people dead in a fire in the Bronx," and her father would ask, every time, every single time, "Space heater?" Even if the paper said that there had been bad electrical wiring, or someone smoking in bed, or a child playing with matches, her parents were certain: put one of those things in your home, and sooner or later they'd be identifying you by your jewelry or your teeth. Luckily the heating system in their building was so enthusiastic that the windows had to be cracked between January and April so that they would not all suffocate. "Those people never learn," her mother always said, as though the poor willfully chose apartments in buildings where the furnaces broke when the temperature fell.

As Rebecca browsed the aisles at Walmart she could imagine what her father would say if she mentioned buying a space heater. "Put on a sweater! Better to freeze! An accident waiting to happen!" Of course she could not tell him, since he still thought she was on West Seventy-Sixth Street. Everything about her living situation would appall him: "They shoot guns? What's with the dog? How can you eat that stuff?" She didn't notice the two women pushing a cart toward her until she heard one say, "That's her." How was it possible that anyone in Walmart cared about *Still Life with Bread Crumbs*? One of the women pushed past her, bulky, somehow sullen, wearing the sorts of clothes she associated with nuns who had been forced to trade the habit for street wear. But the other planted herself in front of Rebecca and stared up at her. She was very short, and florid.

"I know who you are," she said.

"Ah," said Rebecca, as she had on so many other occasions.

"Stop giving my nephew ideas," she hissed.

"Pardon me?" Rebecca said.

"You heard me," the woman said, and followed the other down the aisle, toward small appliances.

"What in the world was that?" Rebecca said aloud, but she had no idea.

WHAT IN THE WORLD WAS THAT?

One morning a large SUV pulled up at her door. "I was lucky to find this place," the driver said. Rebecca's last name was on a placard in the back window, as though there would be a mob of people at the cottage, all clamoring to find their car and driver.

The Women's Art League Presents an Afternoon with Rebecca Winter.

How long had it been since she had done something like this? The organizer had sent her a lovely letter a month before, ending ruefully with the fact that she knew it was short notice and that they could pay only a modest honorarium. Rebecca had almost laughed when she saw the number, only because it would cover the nursing home for a month. Of course she had accepted the invitation, although she knew the short notice meant that they had had another speaker who had canceled and that she was second string.

In her black dress and her dress boots, she felt like a rusty gate. In the car the driver tried to talk to her about this and that, but she was oiling her hinges, thinking of her work, the questions she was certain to be asked, the kind of audience she could expect, preparing to become that public self. She was out of practice.

"We have a lovely turnout," said the woman at the door of the hotel ballroom, which is what they say when the room is half full.

The room was half full. There was a slide on an enormous screen above the two chairs where she and the art history professor who was interviewing her would sit. The photograph on the slide was, of course, *Still Life with Bread Crumbs*. Since the lights were on, the photograph was a shadow of itself, like those old photographs in her mother's albums that had faded with time.

"I can't tell you what an honor this is," said the art history professor.

In the car afterward, passing through Central Park, she thought about how odd it had all seemed. Her old answers about the Kitchen Counter series and its haphazard origins. Her old answers about the cameras she used and the size she chose for her photographs. A combative question from a man in the audience on the difference between using film and taking digital photographs. "The differences are so clear," he said. "I'm shocked that someone such as yourself does not see it." A combative question from a woman who said she thought too much had been made of the "iconography" of *Still Life,* which she called *"Still Life with Dish Towel,"* which Rebecca thought was actually a good name, perhaps better than the one she had chosen so long ago. Language had always failed her when it came to describing her photographs. When she was asked about what she was working on, she was vague. There was nothing she could say about the cross photographs that could come close to actually seeing them.

Only one moment surprised her, when a young woman in a clutch of young people—an art class assigned to the event, after all these years she could spot them without trying—asked earnestly, "Could you tell us the secret to your success?" It had the feel of a rehearsed question, as though the young woman had said it over and over to herself on the subway train on the way to the hotel. Rebecca's answer was completely unrehearsed.

"The secret is that there is no secret," she replied. "That's true of almost everything, in my opinion. Everything is accidental."

There was a long silence, and then she added, "I'm terribly sorry, that sounded a bit like a fortune cookie." Afterward she regretted saying that. She hoped the members of the class would remember the first part and not the disclaimer.

When the event was over she signed some posters, a few books, and an art magazine article, and slipped out a side door and into the waiting car. As she settled herself in the backseat she realized that during the length of the onstage interview she had not thought, not once, about Jim Bates or overdraft fees or the future. She watched the city streaking by. That was what work was for sometimes, she supposed, for forgetting.

She asked the driver to turn west past her apartment building, and she saw an unfamiliar doorman helping someone out of a cab. The cupcake store on the corner had closed; a sign in the window said a Mexican restaurant was coming. She asked the driver to go to her father's apartment, and she saw her father and Sonya sitting on a bench at one end of the building's circular driveway. Oscar Winter had his face turned to the pale late winter sun, and Sonya was reading a magazine. Rebecca felt like an interloper. "Don't bother turning in," she said.

A tourist in her own life, she sank back in the seat.

By the time she got out in the frigid winter air outside the cottage, night had fallen and the entire day seemed like an illusion. What in the world was that, she thought to herself. When she opened the door the dog's eyes shone in the faint light from the kitchen overhead. "I'm back," she said, and his tail thumped once.

LYING LOW

One afternoon Sarah arrived unannounced wearing a red
wool jacket and a plaid tam, carrying a big wicker basket
filled with a thermos of flavored coffee, a dozen scones, and
a lemon pound cake as big as a brick. "I've been so worried
about you," she said, putting down the basket and throwing
her arms around Rebecca. The coffee was strong, the pound
cake delicious, but after nearly ninety minutes of listening
to Sarah talk—about the rising price of coffee, the Starbucks
rumored to be coming in the Walmart shopping center, the
difficulty of getting poppy seeds, the stroke Tad's aunt had
suffered—Rebecca realized something obvious: that when she
saw Sarah in the shop she could reasonably, at a certain point,
pay her check and leave, but that in her own home, or what
for a time was passing for her own home, she was required

to wait for Sarah to run out of steam. And she had so much steam.

"I need to tell you something that I haven't told anyone else, because I know you don't judge, I could tell that the first day I met you, even my mother said, that woman doesn't judge, you can tell by her pictures. But Kevin has been having some issues, and he got a DWI last month. A Driving While Intoxicated. I don't want anyone else to know."

(Everyone knew. They just wondered what had taken so long. A trooper almost always sat in the parking lot of the body shop a block down from Ralph's, picking off the guys leaving the bar and driving so far onto the shoulder they were practically window-shopping. Kevin's drunk-driving technique was a little different; he liked to stand on the brake at the traffic light outside Ralph's, then hit the gas hard so that the car made a squealing sound. "NASCAR Kev!" he invariably shouted when he did this, an effect muted somewhat by the fact that his car was a Subaru Forester. "The guy is such a douche, he had the window open, yelling 'NASCAR Kev,' when he blew past the trooper," said the bartender at Ralph's.

"In this weather he had the window down?" said one of the guys at the bar.

"Total douche," said the bartender.)

"Thank you for listening," Sarah said as she stood to leave. "I'm sorry I stayed so long. Oh, and we never got to talk about Jim, that's another thing I've been meaning to talk to you about but you haven't been in in ages, but I kept saying to myself, oh my goodness, I have to talk to Rebecca about poor Jim Bates and—" Almost as an automatic reflex Rebecca's hand came up, palm out, like a traffic cop: No. Stop. Stop right now. Her gesture was so abrupt that Sarah stopped in midsentence, her mouth still open. There was a faint clicking sound as she closed it, and then she reached out a hand.

"I totally understand," she said. "Totally. It's so hard, isn't it.

I know that. He doesn't come in much anymore, either, but when he does I try to talk to him but he's like—" Rebecca's hand rose again.

"All right, enough said for now. Anyhow, don't be a stranger. That's what my mother always says, don't be a stranger. Tad said that artists go through cycles and I know what he meant, there are some times when I'm making jelly rolls and I look up and it's like, bam, three hours have gone by. Which I know is completely different than what you do, but you know what I mean. He says he needs to talk to you, Tad, but he doesn't want to interrupt your process, he says. Plus he has to drive his mom to the rehab place where his aunt is, it's like the entire left side of her body is dead, just dead." A cold gust came in the door, and Rebecca shivered. The space heater helped, but not as much as she had hoped. "Oh, Lord, I have to let you get out of the wind," Sarah said. "But don't be a stranger. I love your hair like that, too. It's really different."

When Sarah was gone Rebecca looked in the mirror. She realized she hadn't looked in the mirror for several days. Her hair reached to below her shoulders, and she'd taken to wearing it in a stubby braid down her back. She sighed. "I look like one of those women," she said to the dog, who looked as though he understood what she meant, although she wasn't sure what she meant herself. One of those women who let themselves go, who paid no attention to how they looked? One of those women who had given up, like the ones she saw in the market in the city sometimes with their canvas shopping bags, buying one grapefruit and a box of eight tea bags?

A week later she went to Tea for Two for breakfast to head off another home visit, although she looked carefully for Jim Bates's truck before she pulled into one of the spots in front of the place. "Yippee!" Sarah shouted, startling two strangers who had obviously wandered in from the highway. They were the only customers in the place, since it was nearly ten and all the usuals were long gone. Rebecca opened her computer and began to work, looking through some of the images she'd saved over the last several weeks. And what happened next happened unexpectedly, and quickly, and, as it turned out, fortuitously.

DOG PICTURES

Two important, albeit terse, messages in a single day:

"Call me," said the message from TG she opened in Tea for Two. Rebecca wondered if there had ever been a period of TG's life when she had used, or been told to use, or considered using, the word *please*. It was as though TG was stuck in the old days of telegram communication, when each word cost you, and good manners were expensive. I will call her when I have a minute, thought Rebecca. I will call her when I'm next in town. I will call her when I'm good and ready.

She called her a half hour later, from a turnaround on the county road where, for reasons best known to her phone company, her cell service sounded as though she was sitting across the desk from someone instead of speaking underwater. She called her because she thought there might be some money in it.

"Dog pictures," TG said, her voice as clear as a digital recording, complete with disbelief, contempt, and hostility.

"Dog pictures?" Rebecca said.

"Dog pictures."

"Dog pictures," Rebecca replied, with an edge to her voice.

"I'm at a gallery opening in Chelsea and Jackson Meehan from *Aperture* magazine comes up to me and says, don't you rep Rebecca Winter? And I think he's going to talk about an assignment, and instead he says he has a friend who went into some little podunk town off the freeway last month and stopped for coffee and saw six photographs on the wall. Six Rebecca Winter photographs. Six Rebecca Winter photographs of which Rebecca Winter's agent was completely ignorant. If you could have seen the look on Jackson Meehan's face. Six Rebecca Winter photographs which his friend bought, in their entirety, all six, for twelve hundred dollars. Dog pictures."

Sarah had been breathless and pink with excitement and joy. A barter system, it had been, when Rebecca once again began to run low on firewood, this time with no log splitter in sight. Sarah had seen the photographs of the dog on her computer— "I wasn't snooping, but I was clearing and I saw that one, and, wow, it's so great!"—and Rebecca had printed and framed a set to fill the long white empty wall. And then, according to Sarah, a man had come in one morning and carried his mug over to squint at the signature at the bottom and said, "How much?"

"For which one?" Sarah had said.

("I swore it was that one where the dog is looking at the camera and yawning. Because I love that one. Sometimes I say, 'Kevin, I'm going to bring that picture home and hang it in the living room.' Because I know he would love it, too. He's not so into art, or dogs, but he would love that picture. I know it.")

"All of them," the visitor had replied.

What had Rebecca felt, when she saw the wall blank except for the hardware? Astonishment? Distress? And then Sarah had handed her twelve hundred dollars in hundreds, and she was both humiliated and elated. This is what it has come to, she thought, as she persuaded Sarah to take a commission of one hundred dollars, and Sarah promised her free scones forever. Dog pictures.

"Dog pictures," TG said again.

What did it exactly? Was it the fact that the car was so cold that she could see her breath in the air, that her worn parka ripped at a seam as she shifted in the seat to turn up the heat and a squall of goose feathers rose around her, that her head hurt from what she suspected was a smoking furnace and she had had a chimney fire two days before because she had used Kevin's cheap wood by mistake? Was it the fact that she now kept the snow shovel inside the front door in case there was another blizzard and that it fell with a loud clatter whenever she walked past it? Was it that she had spent two days toting wood into the house and from time to time a log roll would suddenly take hold and she would have to stack it all again, knowing there was a right way to do this and she didn't know it, knowing who knew it for sure?

Was it everything, all together, that made her say in a tough cold voice not unlike TG's own, "And your point is?"

"My point? My point? You are devaluing the franchise. A Rebecca Winter photograph has a certain price point. A Rebecca Winter photograph comes with a certain cachet. A Rebecca Winter photograph is handled by this office."

"When is the last time you sold something of mine other than that photograph the Greifers took that you didn't especially care for?"

"That's a problem with the product, not the salesperson."

Rebecca's hair was filled with feathers, and as she tried to speak she realized that one was stuck to her tongue. She picked it off, coughed, and said loudly, "You're fired."

PAPA GONE

The other email showed up on her computer after she had gotten home, trailing feathers into the house while the dog followed with his nose to the floor, sneezing. She took off the jacket in the kitchen, crammed it into a garbage bag, wandered around cleaning up after herself. No money, no work, no agent, but at least the parka had made it through most of the winter, hadn't failed her in December. Her standards had shifted. She looked down at the dog. "Dog pictures," she said, and he looked attentive. He loved having his picture taken. There was always something to eat afterward.

Rebecca turned on her computer and looked through the photographs she had taken of the dog. She would print a new set, and perhaps some other New Yorker would come through, stop for coffee, and buy them. "I think they would make the cutest greeting cards," Sarah had said, as though this would be the zenith of Rebecca's achievement, the way her novelist acquaintances always complained that the public did not take them seriously unless a movie had been made of one of their books.

She had only one email, from an address that looked for a moment both familiar and strange, and then she realized it was from Sonya. When she opened it, it said, "Papa gone."

PAPA GONE

From the obituary column of *The New York Times:*

Winter, Oscar: Beloved husband, father and grandfather. Former
president of Freeman Foundations of New York City. Survived
by his wife, Beatrice; daughter, Rebecca; and grandson, Benjamin Symington. Friends may call Thursday at ten A.M. at the
Riverside Memorial Chapel, West Seventy-Sixth Street. Burial
to follow in Green-Wood Cemetery, Brooklyn.

PAPA GONE

"No shivah?" said the man in the gray suit.

"My father left very explicit instructions," Rebecca said.

"Understood," he said. "His preplanning was a model of the form. For your mother, too. He chose Green-Wood Cemetery because Leonard Bernstein is buried there, which he assumed would please her. But sometimes the family is not in agreement on the decedent's plans and decides to modify somewhat."

He leaned in close and touched Rebecca's arm. "By the by, I love your work."

"No shivah," said Ben.

Sonya looked away. She had no stake in the discussion, being, it turned out, Lutheran. All these years Rebecca had assumed Sonya, too, was Jewish, in the unspoken way in which the Winter family had been, and it turned out that, like her employers' affinity for strawberry jam (not jelly) and shirts with light starch, she had simply absorbed it and used it where appropriate without adopting it at all.

"Family Feud," she'd said to Rebecca the night before at the apartment, pointing to the television, a solitary standing lamp giving an air of dolor to the place and casting the Mary Cassatt in the foyer in deep shadow. "He say, 'Sonya, how come no cherry pie these days?' I say, 'Bakery on the boulevard on vacation, two weeks.' He say, 'No way to run a business, that.' Then he cough, then he fall, then I call nine-one-one."

"I'm sure you did everything necessary," Rebecca had said.

Rebecca looked around the room at the funeral chapel, a living room for the dead or, more accurately, for the friends of the dead. She couldn't count how many times she had been here, although they did redecorate with some regularity. It was currently blue and cream. It had been gold and tan when her grandmother's funeral had been handled by the people here. Shivah had been at their apartment, just a few blocks away.

"Shivah, now there's a racket!" her father liked to say. "Some of them bring food, but what is it? Some little casserole, feeds maybe four people who eat like birds, and meanwhile you've got a houseful. You know what shivah means? Hungry! Shivah means more lox than you can shake a stick at!"

As if he could read her thoughts Ben leaned toward her and said, "You know how many bagels you need for shivah?"

"Hundreds," Rebecca murmured as her son put his arm around her shoulder.

Or perhaps not. Her father had been ninety-one years old. Except for his daughter and his grandson, his family was gone, unless you counted Sonya and, of course, his wife. So were nearly all of his friends, and all of the people he'd overseen at Freeman Foundations until they'd closed the showroom and the factory. Cheap white utilitarian bras, or brassieres as they had always called them at the company. Girdles so snug "you can go down a dress size," according to the slogan her grandfather had coined. For decades it had been a dependable living, a fortune even. And then women had stopped wearing girdles, and started wearing bras that were lacy, flimsy, turquoise and black. The women who wore Freeman Foundations got old, and died, and the sewing machines went still and were sold. "I don't know what else I expected," her mother had said dismissively.

The chairs in the funeral parlor were empty except for a frail couple who had lived in their old apartment building, the administrator of the nursing home where her mother lived, an aide from the home, and Rebecca's mother herself, who seemed to be asleep in the wheelchair, her chin on her sunken chest, her fingers only faintly twitching. The black dress she wore had been supplied the night before by Sonya and was several sizes too large, the darts jutting aggressively because there was nothing inside them. At eighty-six Bebe Winter had the body of a ten-year-old girl. She had had a lifetime stockpile of Freeman Foundations herself, the higher-end Belle line, but none of it fit her anymore.

When her mother had first arrived Rebecca had pushed her chair to the casket, and she had stared at it with a glare so ferocious that Rebecca was instantly in mind of the bald eagle whose picture she had taken several months before. "Those eyes are frightening," she had said and Jim Bates shook his head and replied, "Everybody says that. I don't think he looks scary. I think he looks like he sees everything."

A woman in a dark suit hurried in, breathless. "Sorry," she mouthed, sitting down. She lived in the apartment across the hall from Rebecca's. Ben identified a man in a parka as the unit producer of the movie Ben had just finished. "Quite a crowd," Ben said. Such were the rites for those who had outlived their own lives: a smattering of mourners tangentially related to the dearly beloved, the sorts of people who wouldn't feel the need to make the drive to the cemetery.

"The rabbi would like to start in a few minutes," said the funeral director quietly, and Rebecca nodded.

She knew exactly the kind of remarks the rabbi would make, and as she sat beside Ben in the first row, her mother on her other side in the wheelchair, he made them: Oscar Winter was a good man. (True.) He had been a very successful businessman. (No. Not even dimly.) But the most important thing in the world to him was his family. (True.) He rejoiced in the love of his wife, Beatrice, to whom he had been married for more than sixty years. (The number of years was correct. Rebecca's mother did not even raise her head at the sound of her own name. Rebecca looked at her mother's hands. She was playing the *Moonlight* Sonata. It was one of the only pieces Rebecca herself knew how to play and she recognized the fingering immediately. She had always thought of it as a funeral piece and she wondered whether her mother had, too. "That piece is for amateurs," Bebe Winter had always said when someone requested it.)

Only Rebecca and Ben rode in the black limousine to Brooklyn for the burial. Sonya had refused, sliding into the passenger seat of a compact car driven by a nephew. The nursing home had provided an ambulette for her mother and the aide, and Rebecca was ashamed that her first thought was that she would have to pay extra for that. Ben was wearing black jeans with a black sport coat. She didn't mind, but she could imagine what her mother would have said had she been in her right mind. Even a very fine sport coat, navy cashmere, with very fine gray wool slacks—slacks, she called them, not pants—Bebe considered a kind of shoddy substitute for a suit.

"He was a good dude," said Ben, folding his hand over hers.

"He was that."

"Benjie! Take a look! *The Bridge on the River Kwai!* Greatest movie ever made! Not like that moony stuff you go to see!"

Rebecca smiled. "You do an excellent imitation of your grandfather. He would be proud."

"I'm gonna try it on Nana and see if she reacts."

"Don't wake her, or interrupt her if she's playing."

They drove past a series of bodegas and body shops. She felt a little lost. The driver must be taking a back way. Rebecca could see the hearse in front of them.

"Is Leonard Bernstein really buried there, or did he just tell her that to keep her happy?" Ben said.

"He is. And Jean-Michel Basquiat."

"Wow. That's random. Is there room for you?"

"I have no idea. Nor do I have any interest."

"Still life with urn?"

"Have I told you that you are a terrible smart aleck?"

"Do you know that now they can press your ashes into fireworks and set you off?"

Rebecca raised an eyebrow.

"Too soon?" said Ben, and Rebecca laughed.

The paths wound round and round the lawns and monuments, beautiful lawns, beautiful monuments. Rebecca had taken photographs here once, but somehow they had never come to life. "Do you know a young agent who would like to represent an old photographer?" she asked Ben, staring out the window.

"Are you serious?"

She nodded. "I fired TG. Or maybe she fired me. I took some pictures of my dog and let Sarah hang them in her coffee shop and TG was offended. She kept saying 'dog pictures.'"

"I bet they're great dog pictures."

"They're good dog pictures. It's a good dog. I'm certain you'll like him. But now I need an agent. I'd prefer someone younger. And nicer."

"Mom, this is a complete no-brainer. You're Rebecca Winter."

"I was Rebecca Winter," and her voice caught and trembled, not because of money, or dog pictures, or TG, or her career, or the lasagna that had never ever arrived, but because she remembered how her father would sometimes introduce her: "My daughter, Rebecca Winter. And yes indeedy, she's that Rebecca Winter."

The car stopped and Ben stepped out and gave her his hand and said, "You will always be Rebecca Winter," and she started to cry.

She wiped her eyes as she saw the pile of ocher soil only a few steps from the road, a garish pocket square of artificial grass beside it. She turned as the funeral director's men, in their shiny dark suits and black topcoats, carried the wooden box to the metal stand atop the not-very-well-disguised opening in the earth.

Ben had his arm around her and it was not until she was standing right at the graveside that she saw Sarah and Tad standing on the other side. Sarah was wearing a gray coat with a fake fur collar that was far too snug, and Rebecca wondered if she had borrowed it for the occasion. The rabbi spoke again, vaguely. He read from the Book of Wisdom and then handed Rebecca a shovel. She knew she was supposed to shovel in just a bit, just for show, but she shoveled and shoveled until her arms began to burn and Ben came behind her and whispered, "Hey, lady, give a guy a chance." Ben shoveled for a long time until he handed the shovel to Sonya, who shook her head and handed it to Tad. He was a good shoveler. Then Ben put the shovel into Bebe Winter's hands and pretended that she had helped him put a shovelful of earth into the grave.

"Benjamin Symington, the grandson of Oscar Winter, will recite the burial Kaddish," the rabbi said, and Rebecca listened as her son, who had not been bar mitzvahed, whom she had had to fight to have circumcised—"barbaric," Peter said, but for some reason she would not let it go, it was one of the few things on which she had stood her ground—recited Kaddish in Hebrew. She realized he must have learned it some time before, to know it so soon after his grandfather's death. All those years of being brought up in a Jewish household that never acknowledged being Jewish, and she could remember only one thing about Kaddish, that it included "lovingkindness" as a single word. And that fact she had learned in a world religions class at Holyoke.

("Pop Pop, teach me Kaddish," Ben said one evening after the Final *Jeopardy!* question.

And he did. "Now you can say Kaddish for me when I'm gone," Oscar Winter said. "You want ice cream? Ben and Jerry's! The good stuff!")

When Ben was done he bowed his head, and two things happened at the same instant: Tad began to sing and Rebecca's mother began to—what? Keen? Wail? Or was that singing, too, of a sort, the counterpoint to Tad, who was singing a Kaddish himself? Whatever it was, it rose in the air like smoke and lingered there after the last notes had been sung. It sounded exactly like sorrow.

"We're going to take her back if it's okay with you all," said the aide. "You can't tell how much of this she's getting, you know? It can be upsetting." But Bebe Winter's head had fallen forward again and her eyes were closed, as though she had said what she had come to say and fallen immediately into a deep sleep. "We're taking you home, Mrs. Winter," the aide said, very loudly, pointing to the ambulette, red and white against the greens and grays of the cemetery.

"That was a very odd service," the man who had lived in their old building said to his wife as they shuffled to their car.

"My most heartfelt apologies for being late," said Tad.

"Good job, man. You can really sing," Ben said to Tad, shaking his hand.

"Tad, that was marvelous. Really marvelous. I can't thank you enough. My father would have appreciated it. I would not have guessed that you knew Kaddish."

"I have studied sacred music on a freelance basis," Tad said.

"You can really sing," Ben repeated.

Tad bowed from the waist. Sarah grabbed Rebecca's hands in hers and began to talk in a half whisper. "Really, we thought we would have plenty of time but there was an accident on the freeway, and then it turned out someone doesn't know New York as well as he says he does."

"Our directions were not good," said Tad.

"I'm surprised to see both of you," Rebecca said. "I'm very touched. Extremely touched. You didn't have to come all this way."

"What do you mean? Of course we came. Tad saw it somewhere online and I said, we have to go to the wake, and then he had to explain to me, which was really confusing, I have to admit—you're Jewish?"

"Nominally."

"It's just— Winter? Is that a Jewish name?"

"Winter is the sort of Jewish name a certain kind of family named Weiner adopts."

"Deft, Mom," muttered Ben.

"And your last name is Simon?" Sarah asked Ben. "Is that Jewish, too?"

And suddenly it was all too much for Rebecca, and she began to laugh, a barking laugh that made the men from the funeral chapel turn in surprise. She put a hand to her mouth.

"There's a thin line between grief and losing it," Sarah whispered to Ben. She put a hand on Rebecca's and took her aside. "I'm sure Jim would have come with us if he'd known," she said. "But I just couldn't stand to tell him. I knew you'd understand. The poor guy's been through so much and, I thought, if I tell him about Rebecca's dad it will just bring it all back and he just doesn't need that right now, sad as he is. I mean, you can tell, he's hurting with everything that happened. He's a strong guy, he'll pull out of it, right? But it's gonna take time, and I thought, I just won't say anything and he can give you condolences in his own way, at home. Right?"

It was as though Rebecca were at one of those terrible Manhattan cocktail parties, at which people pretended to understand conversations about events they weren't aware of and people they didn't know. She knew that she should nod, but instead she said what no one ever said at those parties: "Sarah, I have no earthly idea what you're talking about."

"About his sister, Polly. You know."

"I don't."

"About his sister dying, how hard that's been for him, how it's weighed on him."

"She died? His sister, Polly? She died?"

"You didn't know? I thought we talked about it that day I came out to your house. We did, didn't we? I mean, I thought you were upset about it, the way you were acting, so we didn't really get into it, if you know what I mean. You really didn't know? Tad, Rebecca didn't know about Polly Bates!"

"Very tragic," Tad said.

"How did she die?"

"No one knows precisely," Tad said. "She'd been quite ill for some time."

"She died?" said Rebecca. "Oh, no, I had no idea. When did she die?"

"Right after that big storm," Sarah said. "Actually, I think he found her the day after that big storm. People thought maybe that's why there was no service, you know, too hard to get around and all that. Or maybe the ground was too hard, you know? I hate to think about stuff like that, but maybe that was it."

"Oh, no," said Rebecca.

"You okay, Mom?" Ben said.

"It's just broken his heart," Sarah said.

"Oh, no," said Rebecca, as Ben put his arm around her, and as they walked away one of the men at the grave site nodded and they began to finish filling in Oscar Winter's grave.

SHIVAH

After they left the cemetery Tad took Sarah to lunch at an Italian restaurant on East Twenty-First Street at which all the waiters sang opera as they waited on tables. Tad had been taken there for dinner the night before the Rothrock competition by the assistant choral director and his wife, and he had never forgotten it. It was a very old restaurant, with very old flourishes, the kinds of flourishes that had long ago gone out of fashion: tapers that dripped colored wax down Chianti bottles, Venetian scenes in enormous rococo gold frames on the walls (although the food was Neopolitan). Tad had the same thing he had had when he was thirteen, veal saltimbocca. The first taste of the food reminded him of the last completely happy night of his life.

"My heart belongs to New York City," he said.

"I don't get it, myself," Sarah said. "I just always feel like there's way too much going on, you know, and for someone in my line of work it would be impossible, there's a coffee shop on every corner. Plus, have you ever noticed, every single woman is skinny. Every single one. But you could live here if you wanted. I bet you could do three or four birthday parties every weekend."

"I can't say that it hasn't occurred to me," Tad said. "Meeting Ms. Winter has been an inspiration. She is a true artist."

"Well, what about you? You say you don't sing anymore and then you open up your mouth today and, oh my gosh, it's so freaking beautiful, excuse my French, but it is. I couldn't understand a word, you and Ben—Ben, right? That's his name?— I couldn't understand a word either of you were saying but it was so so sad. And the way you sing—wow. Just wow. Really."

Tad lowered his eyes. He was fond of Sarah, but he did not necessarily think she was a good judge of music. On the other hand he had been very touched by Rebecca's words. He had a sense that she was not a woman given to overpraise.

(At lunch with Ben, in a so-called Asian-French fusion restaurant that was, coincidentally, only a few blocks from where Tad and Sarah sat, Rebecca told him the story of Tad's downfall at the competition. "He's no boy soprano anymore, but the guy's a good tenor," Ben said.

"I was so touched that you said Kaddish," Rebecca said.

"Yeah, let's not share that moment with Dad, okay?"

"Understood."

"You okay?" Ben said.

"I really need a glass of wine."

"Because of what Sarah told you about that guy and his sister? That's the guy you work with, right?"

Rebecca nodded. "I feel terrible. I should have known."

"We're New Yorkers. We mind our own business."

"I'm not so sure about that anymore," Rebecca said.)

"I'm beyond shocked that Rebecca didn't know about Polly Bates," Sarah said. "I thought they were such good friends. Not she and Polly, I don't know that anyone was friends with her, she never even came in the shop, I wouldn't know her if I fell over her. Well, you know what I mean, I wouldn't have known her if I'd fallen over her. I meant Jim. You'd think Jim would have told Rebecca. I told you, right, that I sold all of those pictures of the dog she did. All at once, too. She gave me a whole new set and maybe I'll sell those, too."

Their waiter put down two espressos and then began to sing *"La donna è mobile."* Tad hummed under his breath. "I know this one," Sarah said.

As they left Tad picked up the restaurant's card and put it in his jacket pocket.

MORE SHIVAH

Rebecca took out her gold fountain pen and opened a box of pale blue paper she had gotten at the Walmart.

The dog lay beneath the table sighing conspicuously. He had not liked spending two days in the shed while Rebecca was in New York. It was cold, and not what he had become used to.

Dear Jim,
I was so very sorry to learn of your sister's death.

Cold. Formal. She tossed the paper into the basket beneath the table. The dog removed it and began to shred it happily with his teeth.

Dear Jim,
Sarah told me that your sister Polly had died unexpectedly.

Unexpected? She had been told that his sister was sick. Perhaps she had lingered for months, likely to die at any moment, not to mention at the moment that her only brother was with Rebecca.

She took another sheet.

Dear Jim,
I am writing to you

No.

Dear Jim,
Please know that I

No.
In the end she wrote only:

Jim,
I'm so sorry about your sister.
                    Rebecca

Before she could find something wrong with what she had written she folded the note in half and slipped it into an envelope. "Jim Bates," she wrote in her strong slanting handwriting, the black ink harsh against the sky blue, and then she stopped.

She didn't know his address. She didn't know his address. She could conjure the small house with the yellow kitchen, the flowered paper. But she didn't know the street name, the house number.

And so the note sat there on the table, beneath the rounded rock, as each day she determined to get the address, from Sarah, from Tad, from someone in town. There it sat, waiting.

A YOUNG AGENT,
AN OLD PHOTOGRAPHER

"Paige Whittington," Ben said.

"That can't honestly be her name," Rebecca said.

"Don't be a reverse snob," said Ben. "She's the best. I called Maddie, and that's what she said. 'She's the best.'"

"She's the best," said Ben's grade school friend Maddie, who was an assistant to a very prolific painter who was prolific because his assistants did much of his actual painting from what he called templates. "She has a penchant for black-and-white, but she has a few people who work in color. She represents that guy, you know the one, who does the subway cars?"

"I like his stuff."

"Me, too. And she reps that woman who did the egg series. She ripped off your mom, a bit, with those, but she's good, too. Who needs an agent?"

"Just someone I know."

"Ben? Benjie S.?" There had been three Benjamins in their preschool class, and ever after Benjamin had been Benjie S., not to be confused with Benjie C. or Benjie M. In fact three times there had been a Benjie reunion: the assistant PR rep for the New York Yankees, the baby banker, and the second unit camera guy on some film none of the other two had ever heard of or would ever watch.

Silence on both ends of the line. Breathing. A sound that might be Maddie opening a bottle of water.

Then a scream.

"Ben Symington, if you are scouting an agent for Rebecca Winter, Rebecca goddamn Winter, if you are sending your mother to Paige Whittington on my say-so, which, you had better believe it, will make Paige Whittington's career, I want some credit. I want my fingerprints all over this. I want Paige Whittington to know my name and put me on gallery opening lists and send me flowers."

"I always figured you were already on gallery opening lists," Ben said. "Paige Whittington," he'd written down on a sheet of paper in strong block print. Ben had once wanted to be a comic book artist. "Graffiti artist, tattoo artist, comic book artist," his father had said. "How the word has been devalued."

"You're evading," Maddie said.

"I think you mean evasive."

"And again. Which means you don't want to tell me. Wait, doesn't TG represent your mother?"

"She did," said Ben.

Another scream. "I want to be part of this conversation," Maddie yelped before she hung up.

"Paige Whittington reps the woman who did that egg series," Ben told Rebecca.

"Those are wonderful photographs," Rebecca said. "I went to the opening."

"A bit of a Rebecca Winter rip-off."

"Oh, please. There's nothing new under the sun. Do you have a number for Miss Whittington? I'm afraid I will never be able to think of her without thinking of Dick Whittington and his cat."

"Mention Maddie, can you? She's the one who came up with her name."

"How is Maddie? Still applying paint for that old fraud?"

"She sends you her love."

"I've always liked Maddie."

"Don't start, Mom."

WHAT HAPPENS NEXT

"Maddie Becker recommended you," said Rebecca.

"I should send her flowers," said Paige Whittington.

She was a tiny woman who looked as though she was preparing to play Peter Pan in summer stock. Her hair was perhaps an inch long all over, a variegated blond. Her features were small and regular, and she wore leggings and a smocklike shirt in a batik print.

"Toad-in-the-hole? They honestly serve toad-in-the-hole?" she said at Tea for Two, looking at the back of the menu.

"If you order it you will have made a friend for life," Rebecca said quietly, and sure enough Sarah squealed and said, "Oh, New York, right?"

"And my mother happens to be English," Paige said.

"You lucky duck!"

"What's the difference between toad-in-the-hole and sausage pie with gravy?"

Sarah sat down and crossed her floury forearms on the table. "Same thing," she said.

"Got it," said Paige.

Just as Rebecca had realized after Peter was gone that she was living with a mother lode of channeled disapproval in her mind, so Paige Whittington had showed her in less time than it took Sarah to prepare their lunch that she had for many years been in an abusive agent relationship. This feeling had begun when she first called Paige Whittington and offered to drive to Manhattan to meet with her. "Oh, I'll come to you," the younger woman had said, and she had, with a packet describing her other clients and what she would do for Rebecca if she represented her. Her other clients were not as well-known as Rebecca, but their photographs were very fine. And how nice it was, to talk to someone who was enthusiastic and pleasant and spoke in full sentences and had an actual name instead of initials.

(TG had spent a week considering whether to insist that she had an agreement with Rebecca and that their relationship was legally binding. Then she had done an income run on Rebecca for the last three years, and made a snorting noise. "So over," she said, and went out to a party on a hotel roof for a London artist whose work made extensive sculptural use of firearms and grenades.)

"This is excellent toad-in-the-hole," Paige said to Sarah.

"Well, all I can say is, you made my day, my week, maybe my month. It's hard, selling English cuisine in a place like this if it's not a scone, and even my scones are Americanized, to be honest, and Rebecca—I still can't believe I call her Rebecca, did you see the poster on the wall, it's signed, excuse me very much—what was I saying? Oh, Rebecca says they're good scones, but I had to adapt and adapt. That's why toad-in-the-hole is under two names, the real name and the one I can sell it with."

"Excuse me," called a woman sitting at another table.

"Oh, hold your horses," Sarah whispered, winking.

"Wow," said Paige Whittington after Sarah walked away.

"She was just getting started," Rebecca said, eating her croque monsieur, which on the menu was called "Deluxe grilled cheese and ham."

"To be honest, she gave me a bit of breathing room. I'm very starstruck, and a little overwhelmed, and I've spent two hours in the car trying to come up with the right words to convince you to let me represent you."

"What exactly were those words?"

" 'Pretty please'? 'I love your work'? No, not 'I love your work,' I think your work is iconic. I think it has something to do with why many of us feel the way we do about photography, particularly women. It's both accessible and mysterious."

"Oh, nonsense. It's not mysterious at all."

"I have to disagree. Compare and contrast it with, say, the Ansel Adams photographs, the Grand Tetons photographs. You may admire, even love those photographs, but you don't look at them and think What happened next? They have an immutable quality—that's their strength and power. But there's no question embedded in them. There's a question embedded in all your work, that sense of 'what happens next.' And women feel as though they want to know the answer to the question, which makes the work conversational, which makes it female."

Rebecca smiled slightly.

"I'm trying much too hard," said Paige Whittington.

"No, it's simply that I'm comparing this conversation with the conversations I had with my previous agent, which consisted largely of 'No sale.' "

Paige Whittington ate the very last morsel of her toad-in-the-hole. Rebecca thought she must be either a triathlete or a bulimic. Her wrists seemed made of pickup sticks.

She swallowed, then blurted, "This is really bad form, but I can't imagine how you stayed with her all these years! Honestly, when you called I expected you to be completely different, tough and mean and difficult to deal with."

"I suppose I left that to my agent since I can't seem to manage it myself."

"Neither can I. If you're looking for another version of that agent, there are a couple of people I can recommend. But I don't think it's necessary. This new work you sent me speaks for itself, as do you. No one needs to muscle their way into a gallery on behalf of you and this work. And, by the way, this work really *is* mysterious. I've spent hours looking at these photographs, and I'm still not sure what they denote. They're mysterious, and they're unbelievably sad."

"You think they're sad?"

"They overwhelm me with sadness."

"What about those?" Rebecca pointed to the long wall of Tea for Two, where another complete set of the dog prints now hung.

Paige Whittington smiled. "They're dog pictures," she said.

"Yes they are."

She pointed to the one close-up of the dog's paw pad, the one that looked like the gap between sand dunes, or perhaps some odd cacti. "That's a Rebecca Winter photograph," she said. "The others were taken by a different woman."

"I can assure you that they're all mine."

"I understand that. I figured that out. But look at the others." The dog looked into the camera, his head cocked. The dog looked over his shoulder. The dog lay on his back, paws aloft, showing off, playing dead. "I don't know that the Rebecca Winter whose work I know would have taken those photographs."

"Why not?" Rebecca said.

"You've got me there. I'm just an agent."

And that was that. There were brownies for dessert, and Rebecca went home full and contented, and Paige Whittington called her mother from the car and shrieked, "I am going to represent Rebecca Winter!"

"I don't believe it," said her mother, but it was true.

"Amateur hour," said TG when she heard, but she was secretly a little uncomfortable, and that night she went extra heavy on the eye cream, although she was not a woman to consciously make the connection between Rebecca Winter's thirty-year-old new agent and the lines around her own eyes.

And the next day at work Maddie Becker got a huge bouquet of spring flowers. She took Ben out to dinner at an Indonesian place in Brooklyn, and picked up the check, and kissed him on the street outside the restaurant to thank him, and then kissed him because the thank-you kiss had been unexpected and, frankly, pretty fantastic. And then she took him back to her apartment, which in a few months would become his apartment, too.

But that was later.

THE WHITE CROSS SERIES

This series of enigmatic tableaux is both mysterious and heart-breaking. Each is as it was found: some images reflect the dis-integration wrought by wind and weather, but none have been manipulated by Rebecca Winter, who discovered them over time in a forest in a rural area of New York State.

MYSTERIOUS AND
HEARTBREAKING

The opening was in Brooklyn. Rebecca was so hopelessly out of date that she still associated Williamsburg with observant Jewish families, mother and father and a graduated string of children walking to shul on Shabbos, like black pearls on an opera-length strand. She'd never actually seen that, of course, but she had heard about it and even seen a series of photographs. Not very good, she'd thought at the time.

From the window of the car she saw young people in odd and oddly similar clothes. There were many young men in small fedoras. There were many young women in torn tights. Some of them were coming to the opening party for the White Cross series. A young agent begat a young gallery owner, although with Paige, whose forebears had indeed arrived on the *Mayflower* and whose great-great-grandfather had founded the Metropolitan Bank of New York and whose grandfather had sold it to some other bigger bank and founded a museum of Americana, youth was only part of the point. The gallery owner was someone she had known at boarding school; his family was just as wealthy as her own, and his goal as a nascent gallery owner was to get attention.

He'd gotten it.

Rebecca wore the same black pants and kimono jacket that she had worn to the Bradley dinner. It had been only a little more than a year ago, but it might have been forever. She rattled around in her own clothes, thinner and more wiry than she'd been that night. It was almost comical, that she had brought these things to the cabin. The jacket had had a thin coating of sawdust on the shoulders, which she assumed meant she had termites somewhere in the closet. Perhaps now the exterminator would take her on instead of sending her to a roofer. Soon it would all be someone else's problem and she would be in Pittsburgh for the fall and winter. This made her feel no better.

"Gorgeous!" Josef Gourdon cried, his arms open. "Your hair! So Georgia O'Keeffe!"

"I never know whether what you say is a compliment or not," Rebecca said, kissing him on both cheeks as though he was from Budapest rather than Kansas City, where his father had been a butcher.

"Oh, you're so clever! Brooklyn! The hip new place. And everyone is here!"

It was true. Art critics, old acquaintances, lunch friends, art school professors, trust fund babies, a young Russian oligarch's daughter in a short sequined dress with her decorator as her date, a pair of personal injury lawyers whose apartment was designed purely to showcase art with a very cramped wing for their children and nannies, the Greifers from Colorado Springs, of course, and dozens of very young people, friends of Paige, of Maddie, of Ben, of the gallery's owner, who was standing in one corner with a champagne flute and a maniacal grin amid the crush.

"These photographs break my heart," said Josef's companion, a young man so tanned and beautiful that he seemed gold-plated.

"Are you an artist?" said Rebecca.

"I'm an Episcopal priest," he said, and she blinked. "I'm sure you've heard this already, but these photographs are both religious and sacramental."

She had not heard this, but would read it the following week, in a review by a critic who had overheard the gorgeous priest.

She had printed the pictures large, as large as anything she had ever done, and the crosses seemed to vibrate on the wall as though they were three-dimensional. Ben had come with her to see the show when it was being hung, and at the artisanal beer bar to which he'd taken her afterward he had said, with great seriousness, as though he was not her son but a colleague, "This is the best work you've ever done."

"I don't mean to be self-effacing, but at some level I can't help thinking that the artist is actually the individual who arranged these objects."

"Take the compliment," he said, sounding like her son again and eating edamame. "What's going on with Pop Pop's stuff?"

"The appraiser from the auction house is looking at everything tomorrow. I'm meeting him there."

"Sonya?"

"Going back to Poland as soon as the apartment is cleared out." Rebecca did not mention the meeting with the lawyer who had explained that, through some complex machinations, everything now belonged to Rebecca rather than her mother, who had been eliminated from the chain of custody as thoroughly as though she, too, was in Green-Wood Cemetery instead of at the Jewish Home. She did not share the scene earlier that day in which she had gingerly broached the subject of Sonya's claims to any of the objects Oscar Winter had left behind. The house-keeper had waved her off with a lemon-scented hand. She'd been polishing the furniture in advance of the appraiser's arrival.

"Your papa, he was a good man. Very good. And he have a head for numbers. Some people say no"—a glare, and a head toss, which Rebecca assumed was supposed to denote Bebe Winter, the failed family business, and a lifetime of criticism—"but he does. He say, 'Sonya, you buy these with this little money, you make big money. Google, Apple, Toys R Us. Prospects.'" The last word rolled around in Sonya's mouth. "Not all perfect, truth, Kodak not so smart. Sometimes old-fashioned. But the Google? Very good investment."

Rebecca had asked Sonya to come to the opening, but she shook her head and shrugged. "Not so much for me," she said. If pressed Rebecca would say the same. It was her good luck that now she was recognizable, but she could remember when she was young hearing people talk about her work and finding it horrible, second cousin to that old dream of public nakedness. She always liked her shows best when she was there alone, turning in a circle until she was slightly dizzy, before the others arrived. One of the cater waiters had said to her quietly before the guests arrived, "These are fabulous."

"Actor?" Rebecca had asked.

"Playwright," he replied, polishing a tray with a white cloth.

Paige pressed a glass of champagne into her hand. Maddie kissed her cheek. "Here's the buzz," Maddie shouted, since the noise level was high. "It's the new Rebecca Winter for a new generation. Out with the old team, in with the new one. And with work that's incredibly edgy."

"An Episcopal priest told me that he found it sacramental."

"There's a priest here?"

"Everyone is here," said Paige. "I don't think a single person turned us down. Certainly not a single major collector or critic."

There was smoked salmon on black bread, and tiny blintzes

and crab cakes. The Greifers elbowed their way through the crowd to tell her how much they loved the stone wall photograph, which they had hung in the foyer of their house on Tortola. The Russian oligarch's daughter was introduced, curtsied very prettily, said "This is an honor" with not a trace of an accent, or an accent that couldn't be laid at the door of a British boarding school. How strange was it that Rebecca found herself yearning for the cottage, the dog, the empty spaces, the tall trees, the solitude, the quiet? She had been in town for three days, and it was all the same, and yet completely different. It was not so much that her old life had slipped away, that someone else was in her apartment, that she was in a hotel in a downtown Manhattan neighborhood with which she was only glancingly familiar. She had gone to a dinner party in her honor the night before the opening, and everyone had asked, with precisely the same intonation, as though it was a piece of urban Gregorian chant, "Where have you been?" And she had no idea how to respond. In the country? Up a tree? With a roofer? In a completely alternative universe that somehow, sneakily, had come to seem more real to her than this crystal, this Brunello, these men and women, this lacquered room? When she got into a cab at dinner's end, her head a little muddled by the wine, she felt the way she always did when she was traveling, as though she was enjoying the novelty but would be happiest when she could consider it all from the vantage point of home, with her suitcase unpacked, in more comfortable clothes.

She slipped out of the gallery, went outside for air, and stood on the street looking in through the big glass window at all the people inside, their faces raised to one another with looks of attention and engagement, a look she knew so well because she had so many times modeled it herself while she thought of something else, or nothing at all. Their faces seemed to float like balloons above all their bodies because nearly everyone inside was wearing black except for one big man, his head bent slightly, his face only a foot away from one of the photographs, the one of the cross with the snapshot of the woman and the girl at its foot. He wore an old gold corduroy jacket and was almost immobile, and when he ran his hand over his pale hair, bleached almost to invisibility by the gallery lighting, Rebecca suddenly recognized him and moved quickly, back inside. But it was difficult, almost impossible, to pass through the press of people, people who wanted to meet her, to congratulate her, to ask about the photographs, to tell her what they meant, or seemed to mean, and by the time she arrived at the spot where she had seen Jim Bates standing he was no longer there, and as she swiveled around she thought she saw a gold corduroy shoulder pass by the window outside and disappear.

THE FLAG

"Jim, I swear, you have got to go to this," Sarah had said.

"To what?" he said, standing at the counter, waiting for his coffee and his cinnamon pecan scone.

"I swear I'm dying to go myself, I mean, I can't believe she even sent me an invitation, but it's the night Tad promised to take his mom to Bingo and he can't get out of it, she gave him such a hard time about even asking you wouldn't believe. And I can't drive to New York City myself, I just can't, and I asked Kevin, and he was like, we're not going to Brooklyn. I've been to Brooklyn. It's not a place I'm going at that time of night."

Jim Bates had looked at the gallery opening invitation, at the photograph on its front of the white cross and the trophy on the tattered bed of leaves. He read the paragraph inside, then looked at the photograph again.

"Can I have this?" he had asked Sarah.

"Okay, but can I get it back? I want to show it to my mom, just so she'll know I was invited. She's not going to believe it otherwise. I'm sick that I can't go, just sick about it. So can you give it back to me? And will you go? To show the flag?"

But Jim hadn't said anything. He just shoved the invitation in his jacket pocket and left with his coffee. He even forgot his scone.

"That's peculiar," Sarah said.

STRUCK BY LIGHTNING

Rebecca Winter lay in bed and listened to the sound from the attic above her. It was not as loud as it had been the last time, or maybe it was just that it didn't seem as strange as it had then, the idea that some animal was running around overhead, disturbing her sleep. She looked at the digital clock on the table next to her bed. If she squinted she could see that it was 5:40, which was early to rise but not unthinkable.

The dog sighed. Everything about him was so exquisitely sensitive that he could tell the difference between a sleeping human and a half-asleep one, between lids closed and lids opened. He rolled onto his side.

A squirrel, Rebecca thought. Maybe this time it was a squirrel. The day before, after getting back from the city, she had taken a walk around the house and seen an odd trapezoidal piece of wood outside the back door. She'd turned it in her hands and looked around absently. One of the things she didn't like about the idea of owning a house was that she didn't understand how it worked. In an apartment you didn't need to know. The super knew.

She had been so relieved when the car had turned in to the bumpy gravel drive, when she saw the dog emerge from the back shed, when she opened the door to what had become a familiar smell of old woodsmoke, mildew, and vegetable soup. One day she had been out walking and she had wondered whether she'd become a different person in the last year, maybe because of what Paige Whittington had said about the dog pictures. Then when she really thought about it she realized she'd been becoming different people for as long as she could remember but had never really noticed, or had put it down to moods, or marriage, or motherhood. The problem was that she'd thought that at a certain point she would be a finished product. Now she wasn't sure what that might be, especially when she considered how sure she had been about it at various times in the past, and how wrong she'd been. She considered the weight at the foot of the bed. For how many years had she said confidently that she was not a dog person? It just goes to show, whatever that meant. Her father had used that expression all the time. It just goes to show, sweetheart!

"Let's go out," she finally said to the dog, who sighed again and tumbled to the floor.

Small curly shoots of fern were beginning to find their way through the carpet of old leaves on the forest floor, and there was a give to the soil that it hadn't had even a month before. The tree canopy made a doily of the pale blue early morning sky beyond. Maybe the squirrel in the attic, if it was a squirrel in the attic, would leave of its own accord once the chilly spring nights got warmer. Her woodpile was running low and the logs she was using made a kind of singing sound, like happy bees, which she remembered Jim Bates telling her meant they were not dry enough. But she knew she wouldn't need a fire much longer.

"Where is this marvelous place?" another photographer at the opening had asked her, gesturing to the photographs, and she'd been vague.

The dog ran ahead and threw himself to the ground, seesawing his hindquarters through the glossy pellets of deer dung. His fine antennae for human behavior, which had made him capable of anticipating a kick even when it was only a vague drunken notion, did not extend to his current owner's state of mind, and her dilemma about what she would do with him if she returned to her life in the city. For a time she had thought of turning him over to Sarah, to accompany the dog prints on the wall of Tea for Two, now in their fourth consecutive iteration, which had made for a material improvement in Rebecca's bank account. But when she remembered the way Jim's pale face darkened whenever the name of Sarah's husband came up, and the way the man had smirked when he sold her firewood, she thought best not. And she somehow knew that Tad was not a dog person.

(In fact he loved cats and had always wanted a Siamese, perhaps a pair of them.)

The dog disappeared, and she heard him bark once, twice, then saw him circle back and head out again. She followed a deer trail across a creek and then into a clearing, and saw that there was a rough wooden ladder against the trunk leading up into the tree stand. There Jim Bates sat, looking down at the dog and then at Rebecca. She could have told herself that their meeting was accidental, but there was really no point to the delusion. For months she had been avoiding him, but since the gallery opening she had been determined to see him, even if she had not consciously known it.

Neither was anxious to fill the silence with words, and so for a minute or two they just looked at each other. During that minute or two both of them realized, one unexpectedly, one not, that they were furious.

"There's a ladder?" Rebecca said.

"There was always a ladder. Sometimes I use it, sometimes I don't."

"So instead of making a fool of myself climbing that tree, I could have used a ladder?"

"I didn't hear you complaining."

"Have I been pink-slipped?" said Rebecca.

"I'm not working," said Jim.

"And you haven't answered my question. And you owe me lasagna." As the sentence was leaving her mouth she wished she could snatch it back, because she remembered what had happened after the lasagna promise, and what had come before the lasagna promise. But even that was not enough to explain why he had shunned her all those weeks afterward, why he had come to her opening and shunned her there.

"Did you admire the photographs?" she asked suddenly, her temerity amazing and somehow pleasing herself.

He looked at his hands for a long time before he answered, as though he was tracing his old scars. "No," he finally said.

The dog pawed at the base of the tree as though he would climb it, and there was a faint growl of thunder from far away.

"You'd better get down before you're struck by lightning," she said.

"You're a weather expert now?"

"That's harsh. I thought we were supposed to be friends."

"Friends? You thought we were friends?"

"Obviously I was mistaken. Come, Dog."

"His name is Jack."

"Who?"

"That dog. His name is Jack. He belonged to my sister."

Suddenly, horribly, Rebecca felt herself fill up with sadness. It was as though all the sad and bad and hard things, her exile, her poverty, her father, her gallery show, her sorrow about Jim Bates and what had happened between them and what had not happened between them, all gathered together like a weather map that showed red spot here, red spot there, red spots moving slowly together and then—kaboom!—a monster storm. She had to stand still for a moment to gather herself, and even then she was not sure she would be able to speak. It was a lucky thing she was too shaken to look up, because if she had seen the way Jim Bates was looking at her soft and trembling face she would have been utterly undone. And she was undone enough for someone of her character.

Finally she managed to say, still looking down, "I'm so sorry. I had no idea."

"I could have told you it was her dog. I could have told her you had him. I didn't. It's not your fault."

"I meant I had no idea that she had died until long afterwards. I wrote you a note."

"I didn't get it."

"I didn't send it. I didn't have your address. I'm so sorry."

"Yeah," he said.

The sadness in his voice, like a musical note, made her fill up again, so she turned and left. She pushed through the sharp shrubs and the undergrowth, caught one hiking boot in a hole and turned her ankle, scratched her face on a broken branch. When she saw the house through the trees she turned and called "Jack?" and the dog came running down the deer trail she would have taken if she'd been in her right mind.

NOT MYSTERIOUS

Jim Bates knocked at the door an hour later. He walked in without looking Rebecca in the face, and when he reached into his jacket she thought for just an instant that he would pull out a bottle of Tullamore Dew. She still had the other bottle, pushed far to the back of the cabinet, glimmering at her sometimes, meanly, if the light hit it just right.

What he held out instead was the invitation to her gallery opening.

"There's nothing mysterious about those photographs," he said.

"I didn't write the copy."

"But you don't know anything about them, do you? You don't know who put those things there and what they mean, do you? You just took your pictures and you blew them up and they hung them up and somebody will pay a whole lot of money for them and that's that. It doesn't matter, what they mean, whose they were."

From inside the invitation he took a piece of paper, folded into quarters, and when he unfolded it Rebecca saw that it was the list of the photographs in the White Cross series.

"*Trophy, Two Views,*" he said savagely, and then he looked up at Rebecca, and his face was flushed. "That was a volleyball trophy she got in eighth grade. She had a mean spike of a serve. They won every game that year except one against some school that had these giant girls, everybody said they were ringers, high school girls pretending to be in middle school. I was away then but she sent me a letter, with a picture of the team. She won most valuable player. Then she played one year in high school, and then one of the guys called her a dyke for playing, and then she stopped. At least that's what she said after, when I asked."

He looked at the list again. "*Yearbook.* I heard someone at that opening say you never move anything when you take pictures, that all those things on that poster Sarah's so proud of are just the way you found them. If you'd opened the yearbook you would have seen her picture on the front page. They did this collage, and she's the one wearing a crown and a bathing suit at the lake for senior days. Her friend Traci wrote next to it, 'The best years of our life!' She was kind of right. I don't know what happened to her. To Traci. She might be the one who became a flight attendant. Or maybe that was Brittany. She lost track of all of them once she got bad.

"The blue ribbon was track. There were a lot of ribbons. I don't know why she kept that one. Maybe it was the only one she had left. She did hurdles. She tore something in her knee, and that was done, too. Maybe it would have been done anyhow. The birthday card—"

"I'm sorry," Rebecca said.

"The birthday card," he cried, flailing at the air with the

paper. "The birthday card from her mother. Our mother. June twelfth. 'I'm a Gemini, Jimmy, no wonder I'm schizy,' she said. And the picture of her with her mother. Our mother. I must have looked at that picture a million times after, and thought, what would have happened if there had been a whole lot of pictures like that, Polly in her prom dress with Mom, Polly in her cap and gown with Mom. But there weren't. I don't even know if it would have made any difference. The doctors always said it was chemical. I don't know, I don't know if they even knew what they were talking about."

He held the invitation and the list toward her. "You get the idea. Just look at them for what they really are. A really really sick girl walked around here, in her nightgown probably, tearing up her bare feet on the ground, and set them all up, and when she was done she went up onto the roof of her house and she laid down in the snow and died. These are suicide notes. They're not some kind of artistic statement or, what did one guy I heard call them, a struggle between nature and man? I mean, who are those people? They are so full of shit. These are suicide notes. These are a way of saying, I don't need these things anymore, I want to die."

"I didn't know."

"No, you didn't. You just took the pictures and let everybody look at them."

"I won't sell them," Rebecca said.

"What?"

"I can tell the gallery they're not for sale. If anyone has written a check I can tell them I've changed my mind."

"Why?"

"You find it so painful, that I made these photographs."

"I thought I'd found all of this stuff and picked it all up. You didn't get them all, either, you know that? There was one with a hat with flowers on it, and another one with a little plaque with that 'Now I lay me down to sleep' prayer on it. That would have made a good picture, right, *Now I Lay Me Down to Sleep*? They would have loved that one."

"I'll call the gallery this afternoon."

"No, no, that's not what I'm saying. I just want you to understand what you were taking pictures of. I want you to know what they really were. They're not just pictures. They're real. All that stuff was real. The point isn't selling them or not selling them. It's what they mean. Not what the pictures mean, what the things mean. What they meant. What they meant to her. To me, too."

"I'm so sorry," she said again.

"I'm so tired," he said.

"I wish I had met her," Rebecca said.

"What was I going to say, would you like to meet my sister, the schizophrenic? Or bipolar, depending on which doctor it was. They could never make up their minds."

"It must have been so hard."

"It was like having a kid who never grew up and never learned the rules. And every damn night I would check on her to make sure she was all right, and every damn night she would say, 'I love you, Jimmy,' unless she was too stoned from the meds. And I almost never missed a night and then—"

"I know," said Rebecca. He'd missed the night that he'd stayed at the cabin. She reached across the dining table, lifted the round stone, and handed him the small blue envelope with his name on the front.

"Thank you," he said after he read it.

"I should have gotten your address."

"I'm just glad you thought of it." He turned the cheap notepaper over in his hands. "I'm really tired," he added. "I'm not sleeping too well."

"Lie down on the couch," Rebecca said. She covered him with the blanket from the bedroom, and then she went into the back room and took down all the images she had tacked to the wall from the White Cross series. He was right; she looked at each one differently now.

Other people used photographs as a way to keep close to the events of their lives; she had used them as a way to stand apart. She had never looked at the Kitchen Counter series and remembered the days before and after, the grocery shopping or the leftovers in the refrigerator, didn't look at the photographs of Ben's action figures or even the plateau of his baby back and think of which toys he'd preferred (the Ninja Turtles) or when those faint dimples at the base of his spine had given way to the firmer flesh of childhood. She'd denatured parts of her own existence by printing and framing and freezing them. And they'd become denatured even further by being written about, analyzed, lionized by other people, by strangers. Sometimes even she had believed that *Still Life with Bread Crumbs* was about women's work.

She looked at the White Cross photographs again with her new knowledge about what had come before and after them, and instead of static images they seemed an infinite prolonging, as though even now Polly Bates wandered, barefoot, shucking her past in preparation for a foreshortened future, pushing the crosses into the earth, laying down the beloved detritus of her life, saying goodbye: goodbye, card; goodbye, ribbon; goodbye, mother; goodbye, brother. She wondered if the great artists had ever considered this, da Vinci with the woman who would become the *Mona Lisa,* Sargent with Madame X, whether they had ever considered the terrible eternity of immortality. She could not even claim that Polly Bates lived forever through her work. Only her loss, her despair did.

What Jim Bates had said, his voice rough and trembling, had finally destroyed the wall for her, between two dimensions and three, as though at any moment a white hand would appear at one corner of a photograph to reposition the trophy, to straighten the cross. "People seem to find the cross imagery challenging," the gallery owner had said, and she had nodded. Now she could tell him: it was meant as a challenge. Keep me alive if you can.

When she went back into the living room the invitation from

her opening and the note she had written had both fallen to the floor, and the dog was sleeping next to the couch with one of Jim Bates's scarred hands atop his head. She sat in a chair in the dark watching the two of them, and when she was tempted to use her camera she was suddenly ashamed of herself for the very first time.

THE WHITE CROSS SERIES—
THE REVIEWS

For decades students of photography believed that Rebecca Winter would be remembered for and defined by the Kitchen Counter series. But the White Cross series surpasses the images of
domesticity for which she first became known. These photographs, taken together, are her masterwork.

—ARTnews

THE WHITE CROSS SERIES—
THE PRESENT

She sold only three of the photographs, two to the Greifers and one to the Russian woman, whose decorator told her it was a good investment. Everyone was surprised. "I'm not concerned," said Paige Whittington, who sounded as though she truly meant it.

Neither was Rebecca, because of the phone call from the appraiser, and because of the desk. And because she knew that *ARTnews* was right.

(THE WHITE CROSS SERIES—
MUCH LATER

The International Center of Photography is pleased to announce that the estate of Edward and Sylvia Greifer has given the entire White Cross series, the acclaimed series of photographs by Rebecca Winter, to the center's collection.

The photographs will tour the United States and Europe during 2018 and will appear in an exhibition in Beijing before becoming a permanent part of the center's collection.

Jessica, James, and John Greifer acquired two of the original photographs from other collectors so that the complete set of Ms. Winter's original prints could be bequeathed to ICP.)

LASAGNA AT LAST

Early in June, Jim Bates and Rebecca Winter spent a Sunday morning working in the tree stand, and that evening he showed up at the cottage with a tray of lasagna and a six-pack of beer. "It's not fancy beer," he said, as though he had to apologize for it.

"I've always liked beer," said Rebecca, which happened to be true. When his truck had pulled in she had closed her bedroom door without thinking why she was doing so.

"This is wonderful lasagna," she said.

"Mario's Ranchero in Bentonville. You been there?"

"Is there actually a place called Mario's Ranchero?"

He nodded with his mouth full, held up a finger, which was his index finger, which meant half a finger actually, took his time, and swallowed. "Not just covering his bets, either. They make good Mexican and great Italian."

"And you can just drop by and buy an entire pan of lasagna?"

"I do their roof."

"Ah."

"I can't actually see Buddy being up for any free photography. That's the owner, Buddy. He's got pictures everywhere, but they're pictures of himself with famous people who have eaten at Mario's. And by famous people I mean the weather girl on Channel 12 and some boxer who won one fight and lost all his other fights. Those kinds of famous people. You could get up on the wall easy."

"I may not be their idea of famous."

"He offered to put me up there for the roof."

"Did he keep the flag up?"

"What?"

"The white flag you put up after you've fixed a roof. Did he keep it up?"

Jim Bates got up and got himself another beer, and one for Rebecca. "I only did that for your house," he said. "For my sister. I put up the white flag to show her that your house was okay. From certain angles she could see your place from her place. Or she used to be able to. Whatever. She used to get strange ideas about people, that they were spying on her, listening to her. She used to look at your place with binoculars, searching for the bad guys. There were always bad guys. I didn't want her to think you were one of them. So I told her I'd inspected your place and it was clean. I put the flag up so she could see it and know there were no bad guys there."

"It kept falling down."

"It doesn't matter now, right?"

There was one of those long chewing silences, and then they both started to talk, and then they both stopped. Finally he said, "What happened?"

"I don't understand."

"I never saw you after that one night."

"You never came over."

"The hell I didn't! I plowed you out three times!"

"You never came in."

"You never came out."

"I thought you had had second thoughts." Rebecca could feel her face turning red.

"Me, too."

They were both quiet for a long time, and then Jim Bates said softly, ruefully, "He sold his watch to buy her combs, and she sold her hair to buy a watch chain."

Rebecca smiled, and he looked at her with his heart in his eyes, and she looked away. "O. Henry," she said.

"My mother made us all read that story in seventh grade. I thought it was so damn sad, but she said it wasn't. She said it wasn't really sad at all."

He got up and put more wood on the fire, though it was too warm for it, and stopped to look over the mantelpiece. "That's a really beautiful painting," he said.

Rebecca turned in the shaky splintery wooden chair to look at it, as though she hadn't seen it her whole life long.

"I've always thought so," she said.

The woman's dress was white with a full skirt, the little girl's white with small pink flowers. They seemed to be sitting on the grass, although there was no background to speak of, really. Both figures were a little indistinct, but Rebecca, even when she was very young, had felt that the mother loved the child and the child loved her back. It had always stood in for something in her own life, although for her own mother the content had not seemed important, only the provenance. "Oh, a Mary Cassatt, but only a small one," she used to say casually to guests, but she always managed to fit it into the conversation somehow.

"It's not a Mary Cassatt," the appraiser had said sadly. And when he had said it Rebecca had been both shocked, disheartened, and somehow certain that he was right and that she'd known it all along. Of course her mother's Cassatt was not a Cassatt at all, just something that could pass as a Cassatt, just as

"Bebe's a wonderful pianist" was not true. Bebe was a halfway competent pianist. But that must never be said, or acknowledged, or even thought, as though the thought would leap from the mind to the keyboard and run across it, playing "Chopsticks," laughing.

Bebe is a wonderful pianist. She practices constantly, hours a day. She will never stop practicing until she gets it right. Even now.

"But," said the appraiser, "I do have some good news."

"Remember Pop Pop's old desk, the one he always worked at at home?" Rebecca told Ben on the phone, sitting at the gas station.

"The really big boxy one?"

"The appraiser says it's worth four hundred thousand dollars."

"Holy shit!" Ben said.

"Exactly."

($548,000, actually, when it sold at auction.)

"The Mary Cassatt is a fake. It's probably by an admirer who became an imitator."

"Wow. That's mind-blowing, too. Any chance Pop Pop knew?"

Rebecca remembered the arguments between her parents, art doing battle with commerce, as so often happens, Bebe resistant, her husband insistent:

"What sort of people tote up the worth of their own home?"

"People who want insurance!"

"Really, it's so vulgar, some stranger looking at everything. I won't have it."

"It's got to be done. Sooner or later it's got to be done!"

He'd had it done and discovered that the painting was not a Cassatt but had never told her. She'd insisted on not having it done because she suspected it was not a Cassatt and didn't want to know, didn't want anyone else to know. Her parents were like an O. Henry story if O. Henry had been more cynical.

"It's like that picture of Polly and my mom, like you can really feel that they're connected," Jim Bates said, looking closely at the painting.

"It's a fake," Rebecca said.

"A fake what?"

"It belonged to my parents. They always insisted it was by a very famous painter and was very valuable. But it's not by her, and it's not valuable."

"But it's so beautiful, right? So who cares?"

People who know about art would care, she thought, and my investment adviser would care. I care, she thought. But that wasn't true. Because the painting was fake, she could afford to keep it. Because the desk was eighteenth-century American, she could afford to go back to her old life. Except that, walking from the minimalist hotel in which the gallery owner had put her up, in which she had had to call the front desk to identify the workings of the shower, she had begun to feel like her old life was a snow globe, something she'd once loved the look of and then outgrew. Or maybe it outgrew her. Everyone was so young. All the skirts were so short. All the heels were so high. All the eyes were so hungry, so wanting.

"Three of the photographs have found buyers," she said.

"Only three?" he said. "I figured you'd sell them all."

"I suspect my new agent thought the same."

"I have to say, I really appreciated what you said about not selling them. That's not what I was getting at when I told you all that stuff, but it was really meaningful that you would make that kind of offer." He took a deep breath, like he was ready to dive underwater, and then he clamped his hand down over hers on the table, and took a deep breath again. For just a moment, seen with his head down, he looked so young, and then when he looked her in the eye, she could see the wear and tear of life, and sadness. His hand was hard and rough. He was the first man she'd ever been with who had calluses.

"Sarah says you're moving to Pittsburgh," he said.

"I'm going for a semester, as a visiting professor."

"Don't go to Pittsburgh," he said.

"I agreed to go."

"Don't," he said, and he lifted her hand to his mouth and kissed the end of each finger, and Rebecca honestly thought she might keel over.

"Can I stay here tonight?" he said.

"Yes."

"Not on the couch."

"Not on the couch," she said.

"Ah, man, a second chance," he said, his fingers grabbing at her hand, turning it over, holding it hard. "Thank you." And he raised his eyes to the ceiling, to the crawl space, to the roof, and said it again: "Thank you."

A SECOND CHANCE

In the morning she woke up to the smell of bacon frying in the next room. The dog had gone to stand at the stove, alternately looking up hopefully and licking grease from the worn vinyl floor.

"No way, pal," Rebecca heard Jim Bates say from the other room.

"This is insane," she thought, and then to make it more real she said it aloud. It was no more compelling said than thought.

"There's breakfast out here," said Jim Bates, standing over her, his wet hair almost transparent on his forehead.

"It's early," she said and pulled back the covers while he pulled off his T-shirt.

"That bad dog has probably eaten the bacon," she said.

"There's more where that came from," he said.

But that was later.

LATER

Tad got a job at the restaurant in New York City where all the waiters sang opera. It turned out that he hadn't forgotten his early training. When he sang the *Pagliacci* aria dressed in full clown regalia he would weep unself-consciously, and some of the older women would clasp their hands and hold them over their hearts. His tips were enormous.

He lived in a small, very neat apartment on the first floor of a building in Brooklyn with a nasty Burmese cat who sang along as he did, and he kept an herb garden that he shared with his neighbors, who also loved the balloon animals he created for their children's parties. He had even fixed up a young woman living down the block with one of the cooks at the restaurant.

He often thought that he should have moved to New York City years before, and when he went to visit his aunt and his mother he always brought Rebecca either a bottle of olive oil or one of balsamic vinegar. His mother resented Rebecca's influence on her son deeply, mistakenly believing that she had spent months convincing Tad to move to New York. "She tore this family apart," Tad's mother said sometimes. Her sister, Tad's aunt, considered her confrontation with Rebecca in Walmart one of the bravest acts of her life, although Rebecca still didn't know what that had been all about.

Kevin Ashby was found dead, crushed beneath a big tree. There was a chain saw near his body, and it was the common belief at Ralph's that he was trying to cut down the tree for firewood—someone else's tree, someone always interjected, to sell the firewood at some inflated price—and didn't know what the hell he was doing. In a halfhearted way the state police investigated, but it was just the kind of accident that happened from time to time, like a lightning strike or an ATV crash.

Sarah cried uncontrollably for months, but only in the kitchen because Jim Bates told her kindly that it was going to really hurt her business if she did it in front of the customers.

"I can't say I'm sorry," he told Rebecca after they went to the funeral, which was poorly attended. "The guy was pond scum. I remember one night he tried to steal the money from the strongbox at her shop."

"Are you certain it was him?"

"The cops caught him. He said he left some stuff inside, which you know is bull because he never went into the place except occasionally to take a couple of rolls or whatever. He messed up the security code, couldn't remember the last two digits. And the security code was Sarah's birthday. So. There you go."

A year after Kevin Ashby's death Sarah adopted a baby girl from Guatemala, whom she named Alice after Alice in Wonderland, and who she took to the family practice clinic on the same cul-de-sac as the vet's office. The nurse practitioner who examined Alice was a man named, of all things, Jim. He sometimes wore a T-shirt that said, IF YOU THINK A MALE NURSE IS FUNNY, WAIT UNTIL YOU SEE MY TETANUS SHOT. But he didn't wear it to work because he was afraid it would frighten the children old enough to read and to need a tetanus shot. He was wearing it when he came in to buy miniquiche at Tea for Two, where also he took a quick look at a rash Alice had developed in the creases of her little elbows, which he said was nothing.

"What a nice man," said Rebecca, who had been there having coffee with the editor who was publishing her book of dog photographs.

"He's so not my type," Sarah replied, and it was all Rebecca could do not to say two things:

- Jim Bates was so not Rebecca's type, which was more or less the same thing as Sarah's type, which was
- bad news.

Nevertheless Sarah began dating Jim, who everyone called the other Jim, about which he was good-humored since he liked the original Jim, who had taught him how to hunt. Or, as the other Jim liked to say, he was dating Sarah and Alice. Sarah still said he wasn't her type, but she sang all the time in the kitchen while she cooked. "You make me feel like a natural woman," she would bellow.

"She has a terrible voice," Jim Bates said.

"Leave her be," Rebecca said.

Dorothea liked visiting town so much that she bought a little place about ten minutes away, with a big brick fireplace in the living room and what would turn out to be a failing septic system. A month after she got back from Venice—"if I never see murky water again, it will be too soon," she told Jim Bates when he asked how it was—she and Rebecca went to dinner together at Mario's Ranchero because Jim was playing baseball with the volunteer fire department.

"That damn poster is on the wall," Dorothea said.

Rebecca shrugged. "They make a great lasagna."

"You look fantastic. Have you had work done?"

"No."

"It's that man."

"It is."

"How old is he?"

"Old enough," Rebecca said.

"It's the sex."

"I'm happy."

"It's about time," Dorothea said. "How the hell did you wind up with this guy?"

"I don't know," Rebecca said, her mouth full of guacamole. She thought for a moment. "And I don't care."

"What the hell has happened to you?"

"I don't know. And I don't care."

"I'm jealous," Dorothea said.

Afterward Dorothea would say that that was the beginning of her determination to buy a house nearby. That, and Mario's empanadas.

Rebecca's mother had a stroke and could play with only one hand. It seemed to make no difference. The nurses' aides at the home said she would live to be a hundred. They were right.

Ben made a small indie film that won a festival prize. Rebecca was terribly worried that he and Maddie would move to Los Angeles.

"No way," Maddie said at the book party for Rebecca's book of dog photographs. "How could you think so little of me?"

The book was called *An Accidental Dog*. The book party was at the animal shelter at 125th Street. "God save me from dog books," the editor of *The New York Times Book Review* told Rebecca. "But a dog book by Rebecca Winter? That's something else entirely."

"Thank you," Rebecca said.

"I'm told you've left the city behind," he added.

"I'm living mainly in the country," she said. Jim put his arm around her shoulder.

"And this is . . . ?" the editor said quizzically, swiveling.

"Jim," said Jim Bates.

"And you are . . . ?"

"With Rebecca."

"I mean, you work as . . . ?"

"A roofer."

"A roofer?"

"Do you own a house?"

"An apartment."

"Never mind then," Jim said. "Nice meeting you."

"You just blew off the editor of *The New York Times Book Review*," Maddie said.

"He didn't look like an editor."

"What do you think editors look like?"

"Taller," said Jim Bates, taking another shrimp from a passing tray.

STILL LIFE WITH TIN ROOF

Rebecca wasn't sure exactly when she first started to think about buying the place. She thought maybe it was when she had been in Pittsburgh, which it turned out was only five hours across the interstate from Jim Bates's place if you made the drive late at night, knew where the speed traps were, and let it rip on the straightaways. The university had put her in the lovely little Craftsman-style house she'd chosen from photographs, and there were things about it that made her realize what she could do to the cottage, how she could make it homey and comfortable. "Yeah, yeah, this is nice," Jim had said, walking around the screened porch and the small oak-paneled library with his hands deep in his pockets, his head swiveling side to side, up and down.

Or maybe it was when the second year of her lease was up and the architect who owned the cottage tried to increase her rent. From reading the papers he probably knew that she had money now. There had been a good deal written about the White Cross photographs, and the dog book, and there had been a resurgence of interest in her work because of it. There had even been a small item in the Home section when her father's desk sold so high at auction. She still checked her bank balance every day, but not with the same sense of terror. The caution, however, would never go away.

"He's jacking you up," Jim said, stacking wood by the door.

"What if I tried to buy the place?"

"That works for me," Jim said with a grin.

The architect said he didn't want to sell, that the place had too many memories, that it was a big part of his past. Rebecca knew exactly how he felt; she felt exactly the same way about her apartment in New York, which was how she knew that he would come around eventually. And he did.

"That's a ridiculous price for this place," Jim Bates said, but he was as pink and glowing as a spring sunset, and Rebecca knew that he was happy. Sometimes he came through the door and it was still a nice surprise, like unwrapping a present.

"I suspect he'll come down," she said. And she was right about that, too. The funny thing was, she never even met him. His lawyer handled the sale, and when Rebecca offered to let the architect come for lunch and take one last look at the place and remove his keepsakes, he sighed and said it was just as well not to revisit the past.

Inside a locked closet was an old set of Mikasa dishes in a faux Japanese pattern, a box of what appeared to be college history course notes, a photo album with only two photos, both of the house, and some fairly unimaginative gay pornography. Rebecca made a bonfire and burned it all except the Mikasa, which for some reason she decided to use.

That April three bulldozers arrived to break ground on the foundation for a new house, glass and cedar and steel beams, a big open space on the first floor and three bedrooms behind. There was going to be an underground propane tank so Rebecca could have a gas stove in the kitchen. Jim had suggested a tin roof.

"It's good-looking, not so expensive, and it makes a nice noise when it rains. But it's your house, your call."

"I think a tin roof would be so nice," said Maddie, who had a secret she was bursting to tell but couldn't, not yet, but that made her think almost everything would be so nice.

"You could use a new roof on the old place, too," Jim said.

"That's where they're gonna put us, babe, in the old place," Ben said. It was funny, how wary Ben was with Jim. He had never been wary of his father's wives, but maybe that was because he knew they were transient, and unimportant. He could tell Jim Bates was neither of those things. Plus he was handier with tools than Ben was. "He's too damn young for her," he sometimes told Maddie.

"Oh, stop," Maddie always said.

"The old place is going to be nice," said Jim.

"I intend to use it as my studio," Rebecca said.

And that was exactly what happened, after Jim's friends in construction put in some big windows and tore out some walls to let in the light. Rebecca wanted to keep the bedroom, though. She had a soft spot for that bedroom. In the years to come her grandson, Oliver, would sleep in that bedroom and feel very grown-up because the real grown-ups were in the big house and he was there, alone. Although he didn't sleep much on those nights because there were so many sounds, scrabbling in the trees, creaking from above, the lowing of a train whistle. He liked staying there better when Alice stayed there, too, and she did sometimes, to give her parents some breathing room.

But that was later.

When Rebecca looked at the map before she bought the house, she realized that she was acquiring a big tract of land.

Sometimes she and Jim walked it, working out the property lines. Not far from the tree in which Jim's tree stand still stood was a rock outcropping. From the front it looked solid, nature's idea of a dry wall, but for a long time there was an opening on one side, although most of the time ferns masked it.

It was uncanny, how large the cave behind that opening was once you got inside. A man as big as Jim Bates would have to stoop, but a small woman could stand within it. Even with her arms out she could not touch both walls.

Inside the cave there were two white crosses standing against one wall. Beside them were a box of Sheetrock nails and an old hammer crusted with rust. There was also a navy blue sleeping bag with a plaid lining, a worn Bible with a curling leather cover, and a framed photograph of a girl in a long dress, blue with a deep ruffle around the neck and shoulders. A young man in a military uniform stood next to her. The girl's hair was dirty blond, but the young man was very fair. A lacy pattern of dark mold had obscured the picture but still his hair shone through.

One year in December a bear found the mouth of the cave. She slept at the deepest end through the winter, and as she turned, half-conscious, she ground the crosses into pieces, then splinters, then dust. Her cubs were born atop the sleeping bag.

When the three bears left the cave all that remained was scraps of fabric, some pieces of silvery metal that had once been a picture frame, and a few pale spars of wood. That spring the cave collapsed. A poplar fell, its roots were upended, they tore away part of the roof of the cave, the rains came in, and so on, and so forth. Then there was nothing except some fragments in the ground, forever and ever.

It was in the nature of things that this happened, and it was in the nature of things that one day, after the new house was built, and Ben and Maddie had had Oliver, and Sarah and the other Jim had had a baby sister for Alice, Jim and Rebecca found themselves standing atop the mound that remained where the cave had once been. It was in the nature of things that he turned to her, put his arms around her, and let one hand drop to her behind. His hairline had receded a little, and he had a big scar on his forearm where he'd sliced himself against the end of the tin roof and needed twelve stitches. She'd been so upset, the blood, the hospital, but he'd said, "Calm down. Worse things have happened."

"There's a chicken dinner tonight at the firehouse," he said as they stood in the forest.

"The last time we went to that dinner the woman who runs it looked at me strangely. And I've already defrosted the salmon."

"Well, then, that settles it."

"It will keep until tomorrow if you prefer chicken," Rebecca said, and the dog lifted his ears. He was getting older, but his hearing was still good. He knew these words: walk, out, down, off, Jim, Jack, Ben, Oliver, chicken, steak, bacon, and bone. Because of the book, he was a little famous, and the vet kept an autographed picture of him in his waiting room.

"Check it out," Jim said softly, and a line of turkeys ran across the deer trail in front of them, two large ungainly birds and a clutch of smaller ones.

"Turkeys are dumb," Jim Bates said.

"You always say that," Rebecca said.

"It's true."

"I'm sure you're right," she said, and put her arm through his and pressed it to her side.

"Let's stay home and eat salmon," he said.

"Perfect," she replied.

ABOUT THE AUTHOR

ANNA QUINDLEN is a novelist and journalist whose work has appeared on fiction, non-fiction, and self-help bestseller lists. She is the author of seven novels: *Object Lessons, One True Thing, Black and Blue, Blessings, Rise and Shine, Every Last One,* and *Still Life with Bread Crumbs.* Her memoir *Lots of Candles, Plenty of Cake,* published in 2012, was a number one *New York Times* bestseller. Her book *A Short Guide to a Happy Life* has sold more than a million copies. While a columnist at *The New York Times* she won the Pulitzer Prize and published two collections, *Living Out Loud* and *Thinking Out Loud.* Her *Newsweek* columns were collected in *Loud and Clear.*

ABOUT THE TYPE

This book was set in Sabon, a typeface designed by the well-known German typographer Jan Tschichold (1902–74). Sabon's design is based upon the original letter forms of sixteenth-century French type designer Claude Garamond and was created specifically to be used for three sources: foundry type for hand composition, Linotype, and Monotype. Tschichold named his typeface for the famous Frankfurt typefounder Jacques Sabon (c. 1520–80).